Eli's gaze roamed up and down her body before returning back to the one leg he still held in his firm grip.

He smiled at her ankle bracelet. It did something to enhance the look of her leg, made it appear even sexier. He caught one of his fingers in the thin gold chain and gently rubbed it back and forth against her skin. "Nice."

He picked up on her ultrasoft moan and knew she was getting aroused from him rubbing her leg that way. She hadn't seen anything yet. Her response to what he was doing sent shivers all through his body, and caused a throbbing ache in his groin that was so intense, he knew he had to get out of his clothes now or suffer irreparable damage to that part of him later. The way his erection was pressing against his zipper was no joke.

"Eli?"

"Hmm?"

"What are you doing to me?"

He held her gaze. "Something called foreplay. At least the start of it anyway."

"There's more?" she asked.

"Definitely. As much as you can handle."

Books by Brenda Jackson

Kimani Romance

**Solid Soul*
Night Heat
**Beyond Temptation*
**Risky Pleasures*
In Bed with Her Boss
Irresistible Forces
Just Deserts
The Object of His Protection
Temperatures Rising
**Intimate Seduction*
Bachelor Untamed
**Hidden Pleasures*
Star of His Heart
Bachelor Unleashed
In the Doctor's Bed
**A Steele for Christmas*

Kimani Arabesque
(all Madaris Family titles)

Tonight and Forever
A Valentine's Kiss
Whispered Promises
Eternally Yours
One Special Moment
Fire and Desire
Something to Celebrate
Secret Love
True Love
Surrender
†Wrapped in Pleasure
†Ravished by Desire
Sensual Confessions

*Steele Family titles
†Westmoreland Family titles

BRENDA JACKSON

is a die "heart" romantic who married her childhood sweetheart and still proudly wears the "going steady" ring he gave her when she was fifteen. Because she's always believed in the power of love, Brenda's stories always have happy endings. In her real-life love story, Brenda and Gerald, her husband of thirty-eight years, live in Jacksonville, Florida, and have two sons.

A *New York Times* bestselling author of more than seventy-five romance titles, Brenda is a retiree from a major insurance company and now divides her time between family, writing and traveling with Gerald. You may write to Brenda at P.O. Box 28267, Jacksonville, Florida 32226; her email address WriterBJackson@aol.com; or visit her website at www.brendajackson.net.

BRENDA JACKSON

A STEELE FOR CHRISTMAS

Recycling programs for this product may not exist in your area.

ISBN-13: 978-0-373-86228-3

A STEELE FOR CHRISTMAS

www.kimanipress.com

Printed in U.S.A.

Dear Reader,

You have to love those "Bad News" Steeles!

When I introduced the Steeles with Chance's story five years ago, little did I know that I would be writing beyond Donovan's story. But the more I wrote about that family, the more I knew I had to tell you about their cousins—those other Steeles who live in Phoenix. They are the ones known as the "Bad News" Steeles.

There are six brothers. Last year, Galen Steele's story debuted in *Hidden Pleasures.* While writing Galen's story, I just knew I had to write about his brother Eli Steele here in *A Steele for Christmas.*

Eli is such a no-nonsense guy who always thought he knew just what he wanted. He loves his job as an attorney and his favorite pastime is enjoying women. Little does Eli know that he'll become a present for some woman under her Christmas tree. Wow! Can you imagine a Steele for Christmas? Read between the covers to see how it all turns out!

Thank you for making the Steeles a very special family. I look forward to bringing you more books of endless love and red-hot passion.

Happy reading!

Brenda Jackson

To the love of my life, Gerald Jackson, Sr.

This year marks my 16th anniversary as a published author and I want to thank all of you for your support.

To those readers who I got to meet during my book tour this past spring, this book is especially for you!

To my cast and crew of *Truly Everlasting,* the movie. Thank you for a job well done!

For none of us lives for ourselves alone,
and none of us dies for ourselves alone.
—*Romans* 14:7

Chapter 1

Eli Steele's looks should be outlawed.

Stacey Carlson couldn't help reaching that conclusion each and every time she saw him. She had been in town less than a week when she'd heard about the six Steele brothers—mainly from the feminine whispers at the health spa she'd joined. At the time, she had merely rolled her eyes in the sauna room thinking the women had to be delusional. No men could look that good.

She was proven wrong a few months later when she ran into the "Bad News" Steeles at her brother Cohen's birthday party. That's when she met all six of them. All it took was one look and she had to admit they were the most gorgeous men she'd ever encountered in all twenty-five years of her life. And with their Smokey Robinson green eyes, chiseled lips, long eyelashes, dimpled cheeks, sculpted jaws and mahogany-colored skin, they were definitely hotties of the most arousing kind.

There was Galen, the oldest of the group, who'd gotten married six months ago. At thirty-five he'd made millions as a video game creator. Tyson was thirty-four and a gifted surgeon. Eli, at thirty-three, was a prominent attorney in town. Jonas, who was thirty-two, owned a marketing business. Thirty-one-year-old Mercury was a well-known sports agent, and Gannon, who had recently turned thirty, managed the million-dollar trucking firm he'd taken over when their father had retired.

The five single Steeles had a reputation for being womanizers and came with a banner a mile long that warned—*Get pleasure now but expect severe heart-break later.* Stacey didn't find the thought at all amusing while she studied Eli out of the corner of her eye as he browsed her gift shop.

Technically, it was his shop since he owned the space. To be more specific, he owned the entire high-rise building, all twenty floors of the Steele Building in downtown Phoenix. She was a tenant and he was her landlord. Her gift shop was on the ground floor, a perfect location that drew both in-house and outside traffic. It was worth the amount she paid each month for the lease.

The only drawback was Eli's daily visits to purchase a copy of the *Wall Street Journal.* She would open up at nine and, like clockwork, he would walk into Stacey's Gift Shop at nine-fifteen. The only exceptions were those mornings when he had an early court appearance.

With nothing more than a terse "Good morning," he would grab his paper and place the exact amount for his purchase on the counter before walking out with the male scent of him following in his wake and leaving her all but drooling.

Lately, he had gotten into the habit of returning every day right before the lunch hour rush to take his time to browse. She shouldn't complain since he would always purchase something, even if it was only a pack of gum. Still, the fact that he was in the shop was unsettling, mainly because the man was so darn pleasing to the eyes that it was hard to keep her gaze off him. He was so stunning, he could snatch a woman's breath right from her lungs.

She hated admitting that she'd been lusting after him for months. She should be the last person to have that sort of reaction to *any* man considering the fix Wallace Flowers had left her in seven months ago. Even now, it was hard for her to believe that her fiancé had called off their wedding a mere week before it was to take place. He'd told her he wasn't in love with her and had wanted to marry Stacey's friend Gail instead.

Heartbroken and humiliated beyond belief, she had quit the computer programming job she'd hated anyway, packed up her belongings and left Memphis far behind when Cohen invited her to come join him in Phoenix. And it had been her brother who'd convinced her to do something she had always wanted to do, which was to go into business for herself.

After stocking several items on the shelf, she glanced up in time to see Eli walk toward the counter. She pulled in a deep breath and told herself that regardless of the fact he was so brutally male, she would not be attracted to him, especially when she knew better. Eli Steele was a known heartbreaker and she had already gotten hurt by one of his kind, in the worst possible way.

As usual, he was dressed in a business suit that seemed tailor-made for his body, especially for his broad shoulders and all those sculpted muscles. Like the other five Steele brothers, he was tall, six-four at least, and had a suave, smooth walk. No one would doubt the magnitude of his success. He exuded confidence and borderline arrogance.

He placed one of her shop's newest items, an antique brass jeweled picture frame, on the counter. She couldn't help wondering whose picture he would place inside the 5x7 frame. She then asked him the same question she asked all her customers at checkout time. "Did you find everything you needed?"

"Yes."

"Will this be all then?" she asked.

"Yes."

She broke eye contact when her pulse rate increased. Drawing in much-needed breath, she forced her hands underneath the counter to retrieve some tissue paper. "Do you prefer a bag or a box?"

"Box."

"Would you like it gift wrapped?"

"No."

In addition to his good looks, she'd also discovered he was a man of few words, which made her wonder how he'd won all those court cases she'd heard about. His reputation as a corporate attorney was well-known, and she knew he represented several local powerhouse businesses in Phoenix. She'd heard his law firm took up the entire twentieth floor. Regardless of the amount of words he spoke, his deep, husky voice still stirred everything within her.

She accepted his credit card and tried to downplay her reaction when his hand brushed hers in the exchange. She quickly glanced up and found his gaze on her. Had he felt the same sensation or had it been a figment of her imagination? She wasn't sure and at that moment, she couldn't tear her eyes away from his.

The tinkling of the bell indicated another customer had entered her shop. Only then did she break eye contact and finalize his purchase. She was careful how she handed the credit card back to him, making sure their hands didn't touch again, and did the same thing when presenting the sales slip for him to sign.

"Thanks," she said, handing a copy of the signed sales slip back to him.

Instead of responding, he nodded before turning to walk out of her shop. It was only then that she was able to release the breath she'd been holding.

"Good morning, Mr. Steele."

Eli glanced over at his secretary. Melanie Larson was a fifty-six-year-old grandmother of five who had come highly recommended. Her work ethics were so outstanding he couldn't help wondering where she had been all his life. She had been just what he'd needed after his affair with his last secretary had ended badly.

He should have taken his brother Tyson's advice and not gotten involved with Liz Baker. Although her administrative skills had left a lot to be desired, she'd owned a pair of legs he couldn't resist. And he'd made getting between them a top priority. Problems arose when he got ready to move on to the next pair of legs. Liz wasn't feeling it and got downright possessive by monitoring his calls and deliberately sabotaging his dates. He hadn't wasted any time uttering Donald Trump's famous words, "You're fired!"

"Good morning, Ms. Larson," he said as he entered his office. When it came to women he was a leg man. That was his one weakness. A woman with a gorgeous pair of legs could get to him each and every time. Like Stacey Carlson for instance, the woman who owned the gift shop on the ground floor. Her legs looked better than Liz's ever did. Due to that fact alone, he knew if he didn't keep his head on straight—both the one on his neck as well as the one in his pants—he could end up in a world of trouble.

After placing his briefcase aside, he sat down behind his desk. Leaning back in the chair, he pulled the picture frame he'd just purchased from the box. What in the hell was he going to do with it? He could give it to his mother or to his sister-in-law, Brittany. But the main thing was that he'd purchased it with no intended recipient in mind. And why? Because he had needed an excuse to drop by that gift shop and see Stacey again. It wouldn't be so bad if it was just the legs that allured him, but the woman was a looker as well.

He had been easily drawn to her beauty the first time he'd seen her at her brother's birthday party. It wasn't the kick-you-in-the-gut beauty of some of the women he'd dated, but it was the kind that would definitely grab a man's attention. And it had done so, in a way he hadn't been used to.

There had been something about the depths of her

brown eyes, the mass of dark curly hair that framed an oval-shaped face, the smooth and creamy texture of her cocoa-colored skin and what he thought of as a pair of delectable lips. The short blue dress she'd worn that night had fit her sleek and curvy body perfectly.

A smile quirked the corners of his lips. Cohen would probably beat the crap out of him if he knew Eli was lusting after his sister, and his friend's actions would be justified. He and his brothers had met Cohen Carlson around three years ago when he arrived in Phoenix to work alongside Eli's brother, Tyson, as a surgeon at Phoenix Baptist Hospital.

The Steele brothers had liked Cohen immediately and now considered him like a part of the family. They'd known he had a sister but hadn't known what a looker she was until she'd moved to town a few months ago.

Eli was aware of the reason she'd left Memphis. He'd heard the story from Tyson. Her fiancé had called off the wedding to become involved with a woman she'd considered a friend. Although he was certain she'd taken the betrayal pretty hard, the attorney in Eli inwardly argued the point that whether Stacey Carlson wanted to accept it or not, she was better off without the jerk.

But Eli couldn't imagine any man wanting to give up their bachelor status to marry...period. He would admit his brother, Galen, seemed happy enough and his own parents' marriage was still holding strong after thirty-plus years. In fact, they were still so much in love it was enough to make a person gag if he was around them for too long. But he and his five brothers were used to them, and were smart enough to know the love affair between Drew and Eden Steele was not the norm. And he could say the same thing about Galen and Brittany. He knew it wouldn't be that way for him, and to be quite honest, he didn't want it that way.

Eli opened the bottom drawer to his desk. He shook his head before placing the picture frame inside to join other items he'd purchased at the gift shop over the last couple of months just because it gave him a few moments to be in Stacey's presence without being so outright obvious about it. Damn, it looked like he had purchased enough chewing gum to last for the next twenty years. He wondered what she thought of some of the items he'd purchased from her shop. She probably assumed he had been buying gifts for his lover, but he didn't have one currently—and he intended to keep it that way for a while.

He would be the first to admit that the ordeal with Liz had left a bad taste in his mouth. Hell, he wasn't sure if he trusted women any longer. It seemed they all had hidden agendas. He was a man used to romantic entanglements of the steamiest kind, so quite naturally, lately, his mind had begun filling up with a number of horny thoughts. But what could he say when he was one of Drew Steele's boys. Everyone from Charlotte, North Carolina, all the way to Phoenix, Arizona, knew just what a ladies' man his dad used to be before his mother had put her stamp all over him. So in their defense, neither he nor his brothers could help their playboy ways. It was in their blood. Even his mother would admit to that. But then she was known to let every hair on her sons' heads stand up by predicting that just like she'd brought Drew to heel, there was a woman out there who would do the same to her six sons.

Galen had proved her right when he fell—hook, line and sinker—for Brittany Thrasher. And now his brother, who had once been one of Phoenix's number one players, had easily moved into the role of a doting husband. It was enough to make Eli and his other brothers jump off the tallest building in Phoenix.

The only saving grace was that they all liked Brittany. And having her around had kept their mother off their backs. Eden Steele was too busy spending time building a relationship with her daughter-in-law that she pretty much left her unmarried sons alone for the time being. A person couldn't ask for more than that.

Eli closed the drawer and was about to open the file in the middle of his desk when his buzzer went off. "Yes, Ms. Larson?"

"Your mother is here, Mr. Steele, and she wants to meet with you."

A frown settled on Eli's face. Apparently, he'd spoken too soon.

Chapter 2

Stacey glanced around the restaurant and smiled when she saw Cohen. He had already grabbed a table for them and she moved in his direction. He had called that morning asking that she meet him for lunch because he had some important news to share with her. She couldn't help wondering what it could be.

She was proud of her brother, the gifted neurosurgeon, who had kept his deathbed promise to their mother that he'd make sure Stacey got a college education. She knew it hadn't been easy for him with his own student loans but he'd done so without a single complaint.

At thirty-five, Cohen Carlson was ten years older and had always looked out for her. Normally, he was an easygoing individual. The one and only time she'd seen him really get mad was when he wanted to do Wallace in for treating her so shabbily.

"I hope you haven't been waiting long," she said, giving her brother a huge hug before taking the seat across from him.

He chuckled. "No, and I feel bad about hogging your lunch hour."

She flashed her hand to wave off his concern. "It's nice to get out of the building for a while, especially since it's usually slow in the afternoons.

"Besides, since I know you're picking up the tab I get to order whatever I want, instead of settling for a snack out of the vending machine," she added.

He laughed and she loved hearing the sound. She could pay for her own meal but she knew her big brother had no intention of letting her do so. And she meant what she'd said about needing the time out of the building. She was still reeling from having seen Eli Steele again today. She should be used to the man's visits by now, but each and every time he dropped by her shop he managed to leave something behind. Usually it was his scent. But today, in addition to his scent, he'd left a reminder of how he'd looked at her when he'd paid for his purchase. Her stomach was still quivering at the memory of those green eyes aimed right at her.

"And you're sure I'm not keeping you from making money?"

"I'm positive."

She usually would put the out-to-lunch sign up between two and three every day anyway, when the helper she'd hired for the lunch rush left, so coming to meet him was no big deal. She owed her brother big time anyway. When she had moved to Phoenix, she had stayed in his condo a month or so until she'd gotten her own place. And he'd been the one who'd told her about the vacancy in the Steele Building and had approached Eli on her behalf with the idea of leasing the space to her to open a gift shop.

"So what's this news you're so eager to tell me about?" she asked, seeing the huge smile on his face.

With her question, the smile dimmed somewhat. "I consider it both good news and bad news. The good news is that I've been selected as Chief of Surgery."

Before she could jump from her seat in excitement, he reached across the table and placed his hand on hers and then added, "The bad news is that it's a hospital in Florida, which means I'll be leaving Phoenix."

His words hit her like a ton of bricks. But she quickly recovered and replaced her look of shock with one of excitement. She knew why Cohen thought the latter was bad news. Moving meant leaving her behind again. The last time he'd taken a job promotion and moved to Phoenix, he'd left her behind in Memphis and in no time she'd hooked up with Wallace. Well, he didn't have to worry about such a thing happening again. As far as she was concerned she was through with men. It wouldn't bother her if she never dated again.

"I don't see anything bad about you moving to Florida, Cohen. It's a wonderful opportunity and I really hope you're not having misgivings about it because of me."

"I am and that's what I wanted to talk to you about, Stace. I want you to move to Florida with me. You've only lived in Phoenix for four months. It's not like you have roots or anything here," he said softly.

In other words, he was saying she didn't have a life.

She knew it but to have him spell it out for her was another matter. "I have my gift shop and it's doing very well," she said proudly.

The first month she'd barely made enough to make ends meet, but once word got out that she was open, customers began pouring in, especially during the lunch hour. And business hadn't slacked since. And with the holidays approaching and the new items she intended to have in stock, she was anticipating an increase in business.

"I won't feel comfortable leaving you behind, Stace."

"But you must and you will. I like it here and I refuse to let you give up this opportunity. I can visit you when the weather here is bad. I'd give anything to spend time in Florida, Cohen, but only as a visitor. My home is here now and regardless of what you think, I do have roots. I might have come here because of you, but I now have made a life of my own. I like it here."

She smiled softly. "I'm going to miss you and all, but I'll visit. I promise."

He studied her carefully. "Do you know what you're asking me to do?" he asked in a low tone.

"Yes. I'm asking that you respect me as the twenty-five-year-old that I am. I know I made a bad mistake in judgment with Wallace."

"What happened wasn't your fault," Cohen said in an irritated voice, letting her know Wallace's actions were something he hadn't forgotten. "My only satisfaction is that you're better off without him."

"Yes and I'm a lot wiser and moving cautiously. You know the saying, 'I can do bad by myself?' Well, I plan on doing good by myself."

She saw the relieved expression in his features. "And you're sure you don't want to move to Florida with me?"

"I'm positive, Cohen. You still have friends here and I'm sure just like I'll be visiting you in Florida, you'll return to Phoenix to visit."

"Of course," he said, leaning back in his chair as if a great weight had been lifted off his shoulders. And she figured it probably was. Being named Chief of Surgery of any hospital was a great opportunity, especially for someone his age. But she knew her brother was a gifted surgeon. The beauty of it, as far as she was concerned, was he worked hard and deserved it.

"Do you have any idea when you'll be leaving?" she asked.

He nodded. "They want me in Jacksonville in two weeks. There is an immediate need for my presence there and Phoenix Baptist has agreed to release me at the requested date."

She nibbled on her bottom lip. She hadn't expected him to be leaving so soon. "Two weeks won't give me enough time to plan anything."

"You don't have to do that, Stace."

"Of course I do. Like I said earlier, you have a lot of friends here and they'll want to see you off and celebrate your good news. Have you told anyone else yet?"

He shook his head. "No, I wanted you to be the first to know."

She plastered a smile on her lips, determined not to let him know how she really felt. She was missing him already. "Okay, now that I know, I want to work on your guest list for the party."

His eyes glinted with amusement. "You're really going to go all out, aren't you?"

Her smile widened. "Of course. You're the only brother I have and I'm extremely proud of you, so yes, I am going all out."

Eli leaned back in his chair and built a steeple with his fingers as he listened to his mother. He'd heard all of it before, so he decided to let his mind wander. And for some reason, his thoughts shifted to Stacey Carlson and he wondered what she was doing. Usually she closed the shop around two every day for lunch. Had she gone out or had she grabbed a snack like she normally did?

And why did he give a royal damn?

The only reason he knew about her eating habits was because one day he'd gotten to her shop around two, only to find the out-to-lunch sign posted in the window. Through the glass door he could see her sitting at the counter eating a bag of chips and drinking a diet soda while paging through a magazine. He had stood there staring at her longer than necessary. And as if she'd felt his presence, she had glanced up and he was hit with an intense moment of potent attraction. Before she could get out of her seat to see what he'd wanted, he had quickly moved on.

"Eli, are you listening to me?"

He blinked. Knowing he'd been caught, he could only smile across the desk at his mother. There was no need to lie and claim he had been listening. Eden Steele had the uncanny ability to know when each one of her sons was not being completely honest with her.

He and his brothers were convinced she had a sixth sense about that.

"Not really," he said, and immediately felt the heat of her glare.

"Then why did you let me continue talking?"

He raised a brow. Had she really expected him to tell her to shut up? Her? Eden Tyson Steele? The former international fashion model whose face graced magazine covers the likes of *Vogue* and *Elle*? The woman who reminded them often that she'd given birth to six males and for as long as they lived she would always be their mother? He knew that didn't mean she didn't respect the men they'd become because they all knew she had.

But…

And with Eden Steele there had to be a *but* in there somewhere. He figured she should be happy. For years she had complained about not having any daughters-in-law. Now she had one and she was still whining. Good grief! Was Brittany not enough? Evidently not.

His parents had sons who'd appreciated the opposite sex from early childhood. They had grown up as womanizers, all six of them. And it amused them to no end that there was barely a year between their ages. That meant his mother had gotten pregnant every year for six years. Knowing his father, Eli wasn't surprised.

He breathed out a deep sigh. As far as he was concerned, Eden needed to count her blessings for Brittany and be satisfied because if she was waiting for him, Tyson, Jonas, Mercury and Gannon to follow in Galen's footsteps, then she had a long wait coming. A very long wait.

"You don't think there's a woman out there who's

good enough for the suave, debonair and charming Eli Steele, do you?" she asked in what he detected was an irritated tone.

He shrugged. "I didn't say that, but since you brought it up…that possibility has crossed my mind a time or two."

In truth, it hadn't, but he liked getting a rise out of his mother every once in a while. She would go home and complain to the old man, but honestly, what could Drew say? Especially considering the skirt chaser he'd been before settling down and marrying Eden. Eli and his brothers had heard the story of their father's past enough to know he made the rakish of rakes look like innocent choirboys.

"You know what I'm hoping for, Eli?"

He saw the gleam in his mother's eyes and decided not to ask, but then he figured what the hell, she was going to tell him anyway. "No, Mom, what are you hoping for?"

"That some woman comes along who'll knock you off that high horse you're sitting on. And I hope when you tumble that you'll fall head over heels in love with her."

Eli frowned as he gazed into eyes that were identical in color to his and his five brothers'. Now his mother was being downright cruel. He forced a smile to his lips. "It won't happen. I'm more like Dad than any of my brothers. Sorry."

In a way, he *was* sorry, not for himself but for his mother who was hell-bent on marrying off all six of her sons. She had her work cut out for her. She might eventually break down Tyson, Jonas, Mercury and Gannon, but not him. He liked his freedom too much and could never bind himself to an exclusive relationship.

She crossed her arms over her chest. "And just what do you have against marriage, Eli? Haven't your father and I set an example of how good a marriage can be?"

He smiled again. "Of course. I know you and Dad have a great marriage, are deeply in love even after thirty-plus years and are extremely dedicated to each other. But Drew Steele's saving grace was you, Mom. You're beautiful. There's not another woman out there who can make a Steele want to give up his freedom."

"So how do you explain Brittany?"

"Britt's beautiful as well. I can definitely see why Galen fell in love with her."

His mother leaned in closer. "Are you saying you don't know any beautiful women?"

Eli's chest tightened as the image of one particular woman flashed in his mind. He forced it back. "Of course I do. But she has to have more than just a pretty face. She has to have a degree of intelligence." Stacey Carlson's face forced its way back into his mind once again and he pushed it right back out.

His mother straightened in her seat. "Well, I'm glad that at least you're not stuck on just a pretty face. There's more to it than that. That might be what snarls a man in the beginning, but he needs to know the woman has other things going for her than just good looks. They need to be compatible in a number of other things as well. Your father and I have lasted this long because we're also the best of friends."

Eli knew that to be true. His parents were partners in all things. More than once while growing up, he and his brothers had tried pitting their parents against each other when they wanted something one parent refused to give them. They soon discovered Drew and Eden stuck together like glue.

"You do know they refer to you and your brothers as the 'Bad News' Steeles, don't you?"

Yes, he knew but he wondered how she'd found out about it. "Who told you that?"

"Sandra Tompkins. Mercury dropped her niece like a hot potato after a couple of dates and she wasn't too happy about it."

Eli smiled. "If you ever saw her niece you'd know why."

Eden's eyes narrowed. "Then why did he become involved with the girl in the first place?"

Eli didn't respond. He figured not responding would provide his mother with an answer. When she slowly raised an arched brow and gave him a disapproving glare, he knew she fully comprehended the reason.

"Is that all you and your brothers ever think about?" she asked in disgust.

He wondered what she expected. After all, they *were* Drew's sons. They may have her eyes but the looks and genes were definitely from their father. They had the Steele charm and the high testosterone level that came with it. Shrugging massive shoulders, he said slowly, "I can only speak for myself, Mom, and I doubt my answer will make you happy, so I'll plead the fifth."

And before she could respond to what he'd said, he quickly asked, "So, where's your next stop?"

She glanced at her watch and then back at him. The

glare was still in her eyes. "I think I'll pay Mercury a visit."

A slow smile touched Eli's lips. He didn't envy his brother one bit.

Chapter 3

Stacey glanced at her watch. It was seven o'clock already. How had time gotten away from her so fast? When she had reopened her shop after having lunch with Cohen, things had gotten busy, which helped keep her mind off the fact that her brother would be moving away to Florida.

Their father had gotten killed in a work-related accident a week before her tenth birthday and her mother never remarried. The insurance policy due to the accident had helped financially, although it hadn't replaced James Carlson in their lives. She'd loved her father but his death had affected Cohen the most since the two had been so close.

Her mother had tried being both the father and mother they needed and both she and Cohen appreciated that. They had started getting their lives back together when two years later, their mother was diagnosed with lung cancer. Five years after that, she was gone. By then Cohen had left for college and she was sent to live with an aunt in Memphis. Aunt Maggie had forbidden Cohen from dropping out of college to help take care of Stacey. Instead, she'd convinced him to go on and become the doctor his parents always wanted him to be.

And he had.

Stacey sighed deeply thinking of her aunt Maggie who'd died two years ago. Stacey had tried staying in Memphis after her aunt's death and had been content until Wallace had messed things up for her. When it seemed she would run into him and Gail just about everywhere she went, she'd known putting distance between her and Memphis was the best thing.

Refusing to think about her heartbreak in Memphis, she glanced down at the boxes that had been delivered a few hours ago. Excitement raced up her spine knowing her Christmas merchandise had arrived. She looked forward to putting the items up on display next week.

"You're still open?"

Stacey swirled around and threw her hand to her chest. She thought she'd locked the door when she'd closed up at five. Evidently not since Eli Steele was standing in the middle of her shop and looking good enough to eat.

Keep those lusty thoughts out of your head, Stacey Carlson.

Only God and she had to know how she usually failed to do that whenever she saw him. Eli Steele wasn't the friendliest of people and was nothing like Tyson, the first Steele she'd gotten to know since he was Cohen's best friend. And all the other brothers seemed pretty friendly as well. Why did this one have to be so uptight and unfriendly?

"I closed a couple of hours ago. I just forgot to put out the sign and lock the door. Was there something you wanted?" she asked.

She suddenly began nibbling on her bottom lip wondering why on earth she'd asked that. But then why shouldn't she when he was in her shop? She'd merely asked if he wanted to purchase something and was not inquiring about anything else. Then why did his eyes darken? It had to be a figment of her imagination. Of all the women in Phoenix, she would be the last one he'd want.

He proved her right when he said, "No, I just noticed the open sign still up when I know you're usually closed by the time I leave each day."

She knew exactly when he left each day since she would watch him pass by her shop. Usually he didn't as much as glance her way. He'd look straight ahead with that masculine "turn-a-girl-on" strut of his. She'd overheard a conversation between Tyson and her brother once, and Tyson joked about how Eli spent a lot of time in his office eyeing the penthouse fitness center across the street. He'd pick out the woman who could kick her legs up the farthest and she would be the one he hit on for the week.

"I got kind of excited about the delivery that came a while ago. It's my Christmas merchandise," she said as a way of explanation.

When he didn't say anything or acknowledge her in

any way, she smiled and added, "I guess you're thinking that it doesn't take much to get me excited."

If she wasn't sure about the darkening of his gaze before, she was definitely certain about it now. She could kick herself. Why did she say such outrageous things around him? Words that could easily be taken out of context?

And then when she saw his lips quirk into a smile, she almost lost her balance. The man was actually smiling. Gracious. This was the first time she'd ever seen him do so and thought he should do it more often.

Then she quickly decided that no, he should not. A stern-faced Eli Steele was sexy enough. A smiling one was too hot to handle.

He surprised her even more when a low, husky rumble that she figured to be a chuckle eased from his lungs. She felt her stomach quivering when he said, "I'm sure there are other things that could get you a lot more excited, Stacey."

His green eyes locked with hers and she could feel air get trapped in her lungs. That was the first time she'd heard him say her name and the word off his lips sounded almost sinful. Definitely erotic. How had he managed that?

"Do you need any help?"

She blinked. He'd said something else. Actually asked her a question. This was the most he'd ever said to her. "Need any help with what?" she asked, afraid he might tell her.

"The boxes."

"The boxes?" For some reason she couldn't follow him. She was too overcome with the nearness of him—

and that wasn't good. Especially when his gaze was zeroing in on her with such intensity. No man had affected her this way since Wallace. And if she was completely honest with herself, she would admit Wallace had never given her this degree of a sensual high.

His smile widened. "Yes, the boxes. Unless there's something else I can assist you with?"

That question had been more than a subtle come-on. Was he flirting with her? No, he wouldn't dare, especially knowing Cohen was her brother. She figured that was why those "Bad News" Steeles always handled her with kid gloves. They worked in the same building so she saw him more than any of the others. He would drop by, make a purchase and keep on moving right out the door without a backward glance. Now he was holding a conversation with her. He was smiling. And he was looking at her like he wanted to get with her. And this time she was sure she wasn't imagining it.

"No, I don't need help with anything," she said.

He nodded slowly. "You sure?"

"Positive."

He stood there and his gaze slowly ran down the length of her body. It was as if he had X-ray vision and could see what she was wearing beneath her slacks and blouse.

She lifted her brow and figured two could play his game. Returning his stare with the same boldness, she checked him out. Boy, did she check him out. Her gaze roamed up and down his hard, muscular frame, appreciating every part of him her eyes touched. He looked good. So good that blood was rushing fast and furious through her veins. The man had such a perfect physique. Definitely impressive. She wasn't aware that many muscles made up a masculine body. And he was still fully clothed.

She knew she should pull back, accept the fact that the man was way out of her league. But for some reason she couldn't do that. She'd never acted so outright naughty with a man before and she was playing with fire doing so with this one. But she refused to back down.

Dazedly, her mind registered that he was slowly walking toward her. Something warned her that she should back up, escape behind her counter, but she couldn't move. Her feet seemed glued to the spot. Moments later he came to a stop in front of her. She tilted her head back. She'd known he was tall but she hadn't realized how tall until he was there, right in front of her without the counter between them.

"Why were you looking at me like that?" he asked.

How dare he ask her that after he'd all but undressed her with his gaze first. "And just what way was I looking at you, Eli?"

She saw something flash in his eyes when she said his name. It was the first time she'd ever done so. And just like when her name had flowed from his lips for the first time, he reacted instantly. It was as if saying each other's names had demolished an imaginary divide that had separated them. Now with that divide gone, they were headed for forbidden waters.

He hesitated. Paused as if he needed to really consider if he should answer her question. And then, as if he decided to go for broke, he took a step closer to her. She felt her back press against one of the tables.

"In a way I suggest that you don't," he said, bracing against a wall, neatly easing her into a corner and blocking them both from anyone passing by her shop.

Good suggestion, she thought. And if she didn't have that Carlson stubborn streak that would raise its ugly head sometimes, she would have kept her mouth shut. But there was something about the green eyes staring down at her that sent an arousing chill up her body. And then there was his mouth. A mouth that her gaze would connect to each and every time he came into her shop. A mouth that looked so doggone kissable, she could imagine not only kissing it but doing a lot of other things with it.

"You're doing it again, Stacey." His voice lowered and it sounded huskier than it had ever been. His frown should have been another warning. Again, she didn't take it.

She crossed her arms over her chest. There was no reason to pretend she didn't know what he was insinuating so she said, "So are you, Eli."

Eli watched the way Stacey crossed her arms over her chest, making the way her breasts pressed against her blouse a total turn-on. He drew in a deep breath. What in the hell was she doing? This wasn't just any woman he wanted to toss between the sheets. This was Cohen Carlson's sister. He liked Cohen. He respected him. And definitely considered him a friend. The last thing Eli needed was to have the hots for his sister. Too late.

It had started the night he'd seen her at Cohen's birthday party and escalated the day she had walked into his office to sign the lease agreement. He'd heard about Cohen's sister, but hadn't expected her to be such a stunning shock to his male senses. And a part of him hadn't gotten over it or her since then.

She was right. He was staring at her, thinking that if given the chance, a perfect opportunity, he wouldn't hesitate eating her alive. But he knew better. Drew and Eden didn't raise a fool. He recognized warning signs when he saw them. But still, there was something about those luscious glazed lips she was nibbling on that got him right in the gut in the most arousing way.

"It's getting late," she said softly.

He definitely knew what time it was and forging into forbidden territory was not smart. But he couldn't help it. He could stand there and stare her down for the rest of the night, take in all the lushness of her curves, the firmness of her breasts and the beauty of her face. And speaking of her breasts...

He looked down at them again and thought he would love to see her in a clingy T-shirt. A wet clingy one. Better still, he would love to see her naked. "You're a beautiful woman, Stacey Carlson."

He watched her expression and knew his compliment had tilted her off balance. The narrowing of her gaze indicated she didn't like it. He inwardly smiled. She had spunk, though he really shouldn't be surprised. After all, she was Cohen's sister. But beauty and spunk together could be lethal in a woman. And if you threw in a gorgeous pair of legs, then a man could definitely find himself in serious trouble.

"Thanks," she said as if annoyed with his words instead of appreciative. Did she think he was feeding her a line? Evidently she did.

"You're right, it's getting late. The building's almost empty. I'll walk you out," he said smoothly.

He saw the panic in her eyes when she quickly said, "You don't have to do that."

For some reason he liked seeing her rattled. "Sure I do." He wondered what fragrance she was wearing and thought on any other woman, the scent just wouldn't be the same.

She opened her mouth as if to argue with him, then as if she thought better of doing such a thing, she closed it shut. He watched her draw in a deep breath before saying, "Fine. I'll set the alarm and lock up for the night."

Her words should have been his cue to step back. Instead, he stepped forward, which all but put him up against her body, he was so close. Too close. He could feel her tremble and knew it wasn't from fear. It was from desire. Desire so keen and sharp it was dominating his senses.

And in that instant, he totally lost his mind and lowered his head and captured her mouth.

Stacey raised her arms to push him away. She was certain that was the reason she had lifted them. Instead, she found them wrapped around Eli Steele's neck while his mouth devoured hers in the most decadent way. She'd been kissed before but never like this. The man was lapping her mouth raw. This was way beyond anything she'd ever experienced before.

And she could feel every single lick all the way

down to her toes. This had to be too indecent for a first kiss and way too immoral for a last one. But Eli Steele was doing more than just proving what a great kisser he was. He was showing why he was considered one of those "Bad News" Steeles. Why he was one of the hottest bachelors in Phoenix and why, from what she'd heard, women would drop their panties for him in a heartbeat.

Stacey didn't think it was possible but he deepened the kiss, increasing the pressure and doing some outlandish things to her tongue. If he kept it up she would be dropping more than her panties. She could see herself dropping to her knees and—

She forced the wicked thought from her mind when his body shifted and the kiss deepened even more. She felt the hardness of him pressed against her middle. It wouldn't take much for him to hoist her onto the table, spread her legs and have his way with her. And it would be just like in her dreams. Those forbidden dreams of him she'd been having for weeks. The ones that took her from a blissful slumber straight into an erotic fantasy. But she would be the first to admit that those hot fantasies were nothing compared to this scorching dose of reality. Things couldn't get any steamier than this. She wouldn't be able to handle it if they did.

When he slowly pulled his mouth from hers, he had to wrap his arms around her waist to keep her knees from buckling under her. And he gave her time to catch the breath his kiss had snatched from her. Moments later when she was able to fully stand and breathe on her own, he relaxed his hold and she gazed into his eyes. They were sharp, keen and caused all kinds of sensations to overtake her.

"Why did you kiss me?" she asked, as she continued to regain her sanity, reclaim her common sense.

In a voice that was just as serious as his expression, he replied, "Why did you let me?"

She could not have answered his question even if her life depended on it. *Why did I let him?*

"Come on, I'll walk you to your car."

His voice, along with his words, recaptured her attention. "It's not dark outside," she said.

"I know, but there's no telling how much longer you'll hang around here if I don't make sure you leave."

She would have laughed if he hadn't looked so serious. Why did it matter to him how long she stayed at her shop? As long as he got his monthly lease payment, who cared? The man had barely said five words to her since meeting her months ago. And today he had almost kissed her mouth off. What was going on here?

She figured she needed to go home and ponder that question. She would definitely be thinking about it a lot. She was used to calling the shots and other than Cohen at times, she didn't let men boss her around. But this time she would relent and do what he asked. The sooner they parted ways, the better.

"I'll set the alarm and lock up for the night." And this time when she said it, he took a step back.

She moved around him knowing he was watching her every move and feeling the heat of his gaze on certain parts of her. Her pants and blouse failed as a barrier against his intense perusal. However, she was determined not to let Eli unrattle her any more than he already had. So, they had kissed. Big deal. She tried playing it off as insignificant, but as much as she tried, it wasn't working. She figured it wouldn't, not as long as she could still taste him on her tongue.

With the alarm set, the only thing she needed to do, other than grab her purse, was to lock the door. She did both while trying to ignore Eli's presence, which was hard to do. There was no doubt in her mind that women would pause when he walked into a room.

"Ready?" he asked when she slid her purse straps on her shoulder.

"Yes."

He stepped closer to her side and automatically she trembled in response to his proximity. She needed to get herself together. She hadn't responded to a man this way since… She couldn't remember when or ever. But she did know she hadn't responded to Wallace this way.

When they got to the door he reached behind her and flicked off the lights. He then walked ahead of her so she could lock the door. When they stepped into the lobby, she realized he'd been right in saying the building was almost empty. Most of the tenants had gone home. In a way, that was a good thing because if anyone were to see them walking out together they would assume they were an item. Lovers at least, especially with the Steeles' reputation. Should that bother her? It didn't because she couldn't be held responsible for what people thought. But she could be held responsible for the way she carried herself. So to her way of thinking, the kiss was way out of line. But so darn enjoyable.

She glanced over at the man walking beside her. At

first it had been hard to keep up with his pace and he'd eventually slowed down his stride to accommodate her. He wasn't saying anything. It was as if he was in deep thought. Had he regretted his actions?

She had broached the subject before when she'd asked why he'd kissed her and he'd countered with a question of his own. One that she hadn't answered because she couldn't. Why had she let him kiss her? Considering her history with Wallace, why hadn't she been able to resist the charms of Eli Steele when she knew exactly what kind of man he was? A man who wouldn't know the meaning of commitment.

She stopped when they came to her car and she turned to him and quickly noticed the brooding expression on his face. He held her gaze for a long moment and she couldn't help wondering what he was thinking.

She cleared her throat and said, "Thanks for walking me to my car. You really didn't have to do it."

"Yes, I did."

She decided not to argue with him as she unlocked her door and quickly slid onto the seat. He stood there while she snapped her seat belt in place and then rolled down her car's window. "Well, I'll be seeing you, Eli."

He simply nodded before taking a step back. She turned the car's ignition and eased forward. When she got clear across the parking lot she glanced in her rearview mirror. He was still standing there and it was apparent he was going to stand there and watch her car until it was no longer in sight.

She shivered inside, not knowing the reason for his

actions. The only thing she could and would agree with was that Eli had had a profound effect on her. And she didn't like it.

Chapter 4

He should have heeded the warning signs, Eli thought, opening the door to his Mercedes sports car. He slid onto the seat not believing how he had lost control with Stacey. He, Eli Steele, the man his family thought was some kind of control freak, had royally lost it and kissed the one woman who should be off-limits to him.

There was no doubt in his mind that he had needed to pull back and regroup when he first saw the warning signs. But before he could do so, he was kissing her with a hunger he had felt in every muscle of his body. And he knew that even now, if given the chance, he wouldn't hesitate to kiss her again.

And that was the root of his problem.

He had liked her taste. Too much. Had it been anyone else, the remedy would be a simple fix—he wouldn't see her again. But given the fact she spent Monday through Friday, nine to five, inside the very building he owned, that was not possible. Still, he was determined to try.

First of all, he would take measures not to patronize her shop. It wasn't like he had to go there. Although he passed by the place to get to the bank of elevators, he would make it a point to look straight ahead and keep walking. She wouldn't be the first woman he'd kissed and then completely ignored afterwards.

He wasn't concerned how she felt about the kiss. She would accept what happened as an attraction between them that had flared and fizzled. They had made a mistake in losing control and kissing. He had been wrong to kiss her and she was wrong to have let him.

Hell, it was so easy to try and place blame or to come up with excuses for what had happened a few moments ago between them. But there was no blame or excuses. Especially not now when his mind was drifting places and thinking things that he shouldn't. Like how it would be to taste more than just her lips. He could envision himself dragging his mouth from hers to trace a path down her chest to capture a dark nipple into his mouth. Then he would proceed to wrap his tongue around it and begin sucking on it like he had every right to do so.

And he wouldn't stop there.

He would completely strip her naked and then he would taste her all over. The thought of doing so was enough to make his erection press tight against his zipper.

He'd wanted women before but never like this. Definitely never with this intensity.

And that's why he knew he had to take whatever steps necessary to make sure it stopped now. He drew in a calming breath, trying to force any and all thoughts of Stacey Carlson from his mind. Not even Liz had affected him like this. He couldn't recall any one woman who ever had.

He was about to turn the corner toward the interstate to head home when his cell phone rang. He turned up his car's speaker knowing it was probably one of his brothers. He just wasn't sure which one. Besides his parents, they were the only ones who had his private number. "Yes?"

"Come join us. We're celebrating."

It was Tyson, the doctor in the family. "Celebrating what?"

"Cohen's promotion to Chief Surgeon in a hospital in Florida."

Eli pressed the brakes to keep from ramming into the back of the car in front of him. "What? Cohen's leaving town?"

"Yes, in two weeks."

Eli's stomach dropped. *Two weeks?* With Cohen leaving town, that meant his sister would do the same. The only reason Stacey was even in Phoenix was because she had joined Cohen after her wedding had been called off. He should be elated if she left. Her leaving town definitely solved his problem. He wouldn't have to ignore her since she wouldn't be around.

So why wasn't he smiling? Why wasn't he eager to pull over and park just to do a happy dance? Mainly because he couldn't get her or that kiss out of his mind, and the thought of not seeing her whenever he wanted, especially on his terms, was unacceptable. In his mind,

Florida could just as well be on the other side of the world.

"Since he's taking his sister with him, I guess I should be concerned about a broken lease," he said, just in case Tyson started wondering why he hadn't made a comment.

"Will you think of something other than the possibility of losing money, Eli? And for your information, Stacey is staying here. She's not moving to Florida with Cohen."

Eli hit his car's brakes again. "What do you mean she's not leaving?"

"Just what I said, she's not leaving. She likes it here. So don't worry about any loss of revenue. Are you joining us or not?"

Eli's head felt like it was spinning. Stacey wasn't moving away after all? She liked it here? Why was he releasing a deep sigh of relief? Why did he feel the need to wipe sweat from his brow?

He gathered himself enough to answer his brother. "Yes, I'm coming. Where's the celebration being held?"

After getting the name of the sports bar from Tyson, he made a quick u-turn at the next corner. He wanted to know why the hell Cohen was leaving town and wasn't taking his sister with him.

"Hey, Stace, where are you?"

Stacey heard the excitement in her brother's voice through her cell phone. She could also hear a lot of noise in the background. "I'm on my way home."

"You're late, aren't you?"

She smiled. "Yes. I got several late deliveries and I

wanted to go through the boxes. They were new items for the holidays."

"Well, how about coming here? I'm at Ireland Bar and Grill. My promotion has been announced and a couple of friends from the hospital are buying drinks. I want you here, but if you're too tired then..."

"I'm on my way."

She clicked off the phone and smiled. As far as family went, she and Cohen were all that was left after Aunt Maggie had died. And if he wanted her there then she would be there. Besides, what else did she have to do once she got home?

Other than continue to think about the kiss she had shared with Eli.

It was Friday evening and while most women were planning their weekend curled in a man's arms, she was planning to spend hers curled up with a good book. Between the covers of a book was safer than between the bed covers with a man, she rationalized.

At least she had a Halloween party to go to this weekend. It was for charity and she was going solo. She had purchased the tickets from one of her customers and since it was for a good cause, she figured she would get out of the house and have some fun.

Stacey made a right at the next corner, grateful she wasn't too far away from where Cohen and his hospital friends were celebrating. She could just imagine what Eli Steele was thinking about now. Was he assuming that kiss would be the first of many? Was he setting her up as his next conquest? There was no doubt in her mind he probably had big plans for the weekend. Womanizers always did.

The thought of Eli and his arrogance only made her get mad at herself for succumbing to his charms. So why had she done it? She knew the answer without much thought. Eli got next to her on a sensual level. He had the ability to make every single nerve ending in her body chime to the sound of his low and husky voice. The chemistry she'd always imagined she felt between them was very real. They had proven it that afternoon in her shop. And it hadn't ended there. When he'd walked her to her car and she had glanced at him one last time before getting inside, she had seen the heated desire still simmering in the depths of his green eyes.

And her body had responded in kind.

She drew in a deep breath trying to remember the last time she had made love with a man. She and Wallace had decided a year before the wedding to stop sleeping together to make their special day that much more memorable. At least that's what he'd suggested to her. At the time, she hadn't known about him and Gail. He had stopped sleeping with her to start sharing a bed with a woman she'd considered a friend. Some friend.

She had heard from her friends in Memphis that the couple was talking about getting married in the spring. How ironic was that? The woman who had helped to ruin Stacey's own spring wedding was now planning one of her own. In a way, Gail had done her a big favor. She now saw that marrying Wallace would have been a huge mistake.

Just like kissing Eli had been another mistake. She could handle the passion; in fact, she would even go so far and admit that she had enjoyed it tremendously. But sexual pleasure wasn't worth the pain she'd one day experience from a man like Eli Steele. Unless… Unless she could play the game like him. Could she? Could she enjoy passion with a man like Eli and not let her emotions get involved? Men did it all the time so why couldn't she? She'd tried the love-forever-after way of thinking and it hadn't worked. So what was next for her?

She didn't want to sound cynical, but Wallace had definitely opened her eyes. Men were not to be trusted when it came to a woman's heart so why put it in their hands?

Then she thought about Eli Steele's hands. She'd seen them numerous times when he would give her his credit card. They were big hands, strong hands. She could just imagine how those same hands would feel touching her body all over. The thought made heat thrum slowly through her, made her nipples strain tight against her blouse.

She forced all thoughts of Eli from her mind when she reached Ireland, a local hangout near the hospital. She was determined that no matter how sad she was about Cohen leaving, she would put a smile on. She had no choice.

Eli knew the moment Stacey entered the restaurant. It wasn't just the scent of her perfume that gave her away. It was as if he had a built-in radar where she was concerned. He had been talking to his brother, Jonas, when he'd lifted his glass to take a sip of his drink and glanced across the room. Their gazes connected when they saw each other at the same time. He could tell she was surprised to see him there. He hadn't expected to see her, either. He could tell by her expression that his presence was affecting her, just as hers was affecting him.

"I see Stacey has arrived," Jonas said, recapturing his attention.

He glanced back over at his brother. "You knew she was coming?"

If Jonas thought the question odd, he didn't let on. "Yes, I was with Cohen when he called her. She was on her way home."

Jonas then looked at him and lifted a brow. "Is she behind in her lease payments or something?"

Eli frowned. "No."

"They why do you have a problem with her being here?"

Eli thought Jonas was too perceptive for his own good. "What makes you think I have a problem with her being here?"

Jonas, the Steele brother who was barely a year younger than him and who had eyes that were shrewd and assessing, tossed him a sly grin. "Because I know you, Eli. I didn't miss your reaction when you saw Stacey walk in. It was as if you'd preferred being somewhere else."

In a way, Jonas was right. But what his brother didn't know was that he really preferred being someplace else with Stacey. And that was the crux of his problem. "Well, you read me wrong. I don't have a problem with her being here. Why would I?"

Jonas chuckled. "I don't know how your mind works, Eli, and I truly don't want to know. But all I have to say is that if Stacey is lodged anywhere in that brain of yours, get her out of it. I heard that Cohen asked Tyson to look out for her after he leaves town, and you know what that means. If Tyson even thinks you're sniffing behind Cohen's sister he will kick your you-know-what."

There was no doubt in Eli's mind what Jonas said was true. Tyson could get possessive when something was left in his protective custody. To change the subject, Eli got Jonas talking about the marketing firm he owned and the initiatives that Jonas's firm was presently working on.

Eli and his brothers were successful and they had their parents to thank for that. His father had started a trucking company years ago—the same company his brother, Gannon, now ran. Tyson was the doctor in the family and Mercury was the former NFL quarterback turned sports agent. Galen had made his millions creating video games.

Although Eli was hearing what Jonas was saying, he really wasn't listening. His attention was drawn to Stacey as she stood across the room talking to Roland Whiterspoon, another doctor at the hospital where Tyson and Cohen worked. He wondered what the hell that was about when everyone knew Whiterspoon's reputation as a womanizer.

Eli refused to even consider that his opinion of the man's exploits was like the pot calling the kettle black. It was the principle of the thing. He knew how far to take things with Stacey, whereas Roland wouldn't care one iota. Then again, was kissing her like he'd done earlier today knowing how far to take things? Had he crossed the line? Was he any better than the likes of Whiterspoon?

Still…he'd never cared much for Whiterspoon and the thought of her spending any amount of time in the man's presence annoyed the hell out of him.

"What's this I hear about you wanting to run for president of Phoenix's Business Council?"

Eli took a sip of his drink. He had been a member of Phoenix's elite group of businessmen for years—right after opening his first law practice. He figured it was time to step up and do more than just sit on the sidelines. He had everything going for him. He was an astute businessman who owned a sky-rise in downtown Phoenix, he was on the board of several local companies and he was known to chair numerous charitable fundraisers each year. As far as he was concerned, that presidency position all but had his name stamped all over it. The other man who was interested, Samuel Nesbitt, didn't have nearly as much going for him as Eli felt that he had.

"Yes, but running is just a formality since I feel certain I've got it in the bag. Over the years I've done everything I needed to do to stay in good standing with the other local businessmen. All you need to do is make plans to attend my inauguration party."

"Pretty damn sure of yourself, aren't you?" Jonas asked, rolling his eyes.

"And there's no reason why I shouldn't be," Eli said smoothly. "Like I said, I've been eyeing that position for years. I'm the best person for the job and they all know it."

Jonas laughed. "You don't have a short supply of confidence, do you?"

Eli took a sip of his drink, deciding not to waste his time acknowledging what Jonas had said. Instead, he fixed his gaze on Stacey when she walked off from Whiterspoon to head toward the snacks table. The owner of Ireland had given them a private room. And because most in attendance were some of the man's most loyal customers from the hospital, he had even prepared a tray of finger sandwiches for them.

"Excuse me a minute, will you?" he said, already moving away and not waiting for his brother's reply. He needed to talk to Stacey. He wasn't sure what he would say to her when he did talk to her. But as he crossed the room toward her, he knew he would think of something.

The closer he got, the more he realized that, except for what he'd been able to glean from his brothers without them getting suspicious, he knew very little about Stacey Carlson. And for some reason, which he didn't fully understand, he intended to remedy that.

He was headed in her direction.

She felt her hand holding the small plate of food begin to tremble and forced her composure to strengthen. After all, Eli Steele was just a man. But what a man he was.

Not able to resist a moment longer, she released a deep sigh and then turned her head to look at him. The features returning her stare were so intense they almost took her breath away.

She met Eli's steady gaze when he approached her, grabbing his own plate to fill it as if he hadn't deliberately sought her out. "I'm surprised to see you here, Stacey."

She heard something in his voice. Was it an arrogant gloat? After the kiss they'd shared, had he expected her to go home and daydream about it? Hide out behind locked doors and pant until the next time she saw him?

"I'm surprised to see you here as well, Eli," she decided to say. She'd bit into a tasty sandwich earlier but nothing, she thought, was tastier than her memory of his kiss.

"I get around," was his quick comeback.

"So do I," was hers.

He chuckled dryly. "Why do I feel that we've gotten off to a bad start?"

She wondered why he was trying to make it seem as if they hadn't met months ago or hadn't kissed earlier. The attraction had been there in the beginning. She would even admit feeling more than a tinge of something that night at Cohen's birthday party when they'd been introduced. At least she could definitely claim that was when he'd begun invading her dreams.

She inclined her head. "And what makes you think we've gotten off to a bad start?"

He smiled, as if admiring the little bit of spunk she was trying to bolster. That was good, she thought. He didn't have to know that although she might be trying to display a tough facade, she was all mushy inside and was somewhat annoyed by the vulnerability she felt around him. And it was the type of weakness and defenselessness she had no business feeling around any man. All it took was a memory of what Wallace had done to remind her that all men were a liability she could do without.

But Eli was different. Not only was he different, he was even more dangerous than any man she'd ever known. Never before had she been so attracted to a man, desired him so much. She was even entertaining thoughts of getting into his pants and ruffling his usually cool demeanor. Thinking about how fine he was could make her pant for days, but actually seeing him in the flesh would be enough to give a woman heart failure.

"Us getting off to a bad start was just my take on things," he said quietly.

"Then let me assure you that your take is wrong."

He looked at her and she wished he hadn't done that. The last thing she needed was for those green eyes to be trained directly on her. "Possibly," he said softly. "But you know very well why I think that way."

Yes, she knew. But she needed to make him think, get him to assume what would go down as the best kiss of her life was nothing she intended to lose sleep over. "Then rest assured you shouldn't think that way. It was only a kiss."

He didn't have to know it had been a kiss with the power to curl her toes and make her stomach quiver. The less Eli Steele knew of her innermost reactions to him, the better. He didn't have to know that even now, despite his reputation, she wouldn't mind going somewhere to jump his bones.

He moved closer, as if he wanted to try one of the sandwiches on the tray in front of her. Instead, he leaned into her and his thick-lashed green eyes made her heat up all over. In a low, gruff voice, he said, “I’d love to prove it was more than that, Stacey. And let me give you fair warning that one day, I will.”

Chapter 5

It was Wednesday morning and Stacey had just finished waiting on the last of her early morning customers when her cell phone rang. She smiled when she recognized the name showing up on her caller ID. It was Deidre Lewis, the woman who'd been her closest girl-pal since high school.

She clicked on the line. "Hey, what's going on, Dee?"

In return she got her friend's warm, vibrant laugh, with the smile Stacey knew she could not see. "Not a thing, but if little Tommy Fielder pulls Melissa Simpkins's hair one more time to cause her to cry, I'm going to give him a taste of his own medicine and pull his."

Stacey couldn't help but laugh. Dee was a kindergarten teacher who enjoyed sharing her students' escapades with Stacey. "Hey, watch it. That might be true love budding. Twenty years from now Tommy just might be Melissa's husband. Don't you know that's what little boys do when they want to get little girls' attention?"

"Whatever. All I know is his hair pulling strategy is getting on my nerves."

Stacey couldn't help but grin, grateful for Dee's call. Her best friend was one of the few people who could get her out of a funk and she hated to admit she was definitely in one. Especially since it was past ten and Eli hadn't been to her shop. In fact, he hadn't dropped by in three days. She'd seen him stroll past without glancing her way. With a newspaper in his hand.

The loss of sales didn't bother her as much as the fact that after plying her lips off last Friday, he could so easily dismiss her.

"I called to make sure you're still coming to my parents' anniversary party," Dee said, reclaiming her attention.

Stacey smiled thinking Dee's parents were the greatest. Back in high school she had made their house her second home and whenever her aunt had to travel or work late, that was where Stacey would stay. "Of course I plan on being there," she said, chuckling. It would be the couple's fortieth year together and Dee and her two brothers were planning a celebration the first weekend in December. "Any reason I shouldn't?"

Dee paused longer than needed and Stacey suddenly felt the hairs on her neck stand up and wasn't surprised when Dee said, "It seems Wallace is coming. And he's bringing Gail with him."

Stacey leaned against the counter thinking about her ex-fiancé and her ex-friend. "Umm, in that case…"

"Don't you dare change your mind about coming,

Stace. If Wallace and Gail being there will make you feel uncomfortable then I'll talk to my parents about not—"

"Don't you dare talk to your parents." Stacey knew the Lewises felt bad about how Wallace had treated her since they were the ones who'd introduced them. Wallace was the son of one of Mr. Lewis's college friends who'd moved to Memphis. Since Dee had been dating some guy named Eric at the time, Mr. Lewis had introduced Wallace to Stacey. They hit it off immediately and the rest, like they say, was history.

"Regardless of how Wallace treated me in the end, he's still the son of your father's close friend," she said.

"And you don't care that he'll be there with Gail?" Dee asked.

"Of course I'll care since the both of them deceived me, but I've gotten over it." At least she tried convincing herself that she had—during her better days. Unfortunately, today wasn't one of them and she blamed Eli Steele. The nerve of the man to kiss her senseless one day and treat her like she didn't exist the next.

"You know what you should do, Stace? What would serve both Wallace and Gail right?"

She knew that tone of Dee's. It meant she had a plan up her sleeve that would do neither of them any good. "No, what should I do?"

"Show up with your own date, a hottie of the most intense kind. That would make Gail see that you've moved on to something a whole lot better."

Stacey laughed. She couldn't help but like Dee's idea. She would do it in a heartbeat if she had a date she could take to Memphis with her. "That sounds like a plan but I don't have a date, especially one who's a hottie." She quickly pushed the vision of Eli Steele from her mind.

"What about one of those hot-looking guys that were at Cohen's birthday party? There were plenty of them and one group in particular I vividly recall were those guys with the green eyes. You said they were brothers and close friends of Cohen."

Stacey smiled, remembering Dee's interest in the "Bad News" Steeles that night. Her friend had flown in for Cohen's party and had seen Eli and his brothers. Like her, Dee had spent most of the evening salivating over what gorgeous hunks they were. Never had she been to a gathering with so much fine male testosterone in one place.

"The five guys you're talking about are the Steeles. The oldest one is married so he doesn't count." There was no need to mention to Dee that recently she'd had the pleasure of locking lips with one of them. "And before you make any of your far-out suggestions, the answer is no. I couldn't ask one of them to go to Memphis with me and pretend to be my fiancé."

"Why not? They are friends with Cohen and seem like the sort of guys who'd like having a little fun—especially if it's to set both Wallace and Gail back a notch."

The thought of doing something like that made Stacey smile. If only it would be that easy.

"What would it hurt, Stace?"

If only her friend knew. She saw an involvement of any kind with a man like Eli Steele a heartbreak just waiting to happen. "They're successful businessmen who have more to do with their time than play a game of pretend with me."

She changed the subject when she told Dee about Cohen's promotion and that he would be moving to Florida. Dee didn't say anything for a minute and Stacey knew why. Dee had been in love with Cohen forever—at least since high school. And although Dee nor Cohen ever let on, Stacey had a feeling something had happened between them at one time or another. She never asked and Dee never told.

"Hey, if you don't want to move with Cohen to Florida, you might as well pack your bags and return to Memphis," Dee said, interrupting her thoughts. "At least we're closer to Florida than Arizona."

Stacey knew that was true but there was something holding her here. Exactly what, she wasn't sure. All she knew was that she wanted to make Phoenix her home. "Yes, but this is my home now. I truly like it here."

"Okay, but I think you not wanting to move back here has everything to do with Wallace and Gail. I understand why you'd want to distance yourself from them, but it's been almost seven months."

"Trust me, I know how long it's been and I've moved on with my life here in Phoenix. The thought of those two together doesn't hurt like it used to." And she truly meant that. In her opinion, their deceitful behinds deserved each other.

"I'm glad. And I hope you'll consider my suggestion about bringing one of those gorgeous hunks with you to my parents' anniversary party. It would serve Wallace and Gail right to see you're happy and have moved on with your life."

Dee had a point there, but unfortunately Stacey knew she didn't have the means—specifically the man—to pull such a thing off. The image of Eli Steele flashed into her mind once again and she could only wish.

Eli glared at the man standing across from his desk. Lexander Stone was another well-known businessman in town and someone Eli considered one of his closest friends. They had gone to high school and college together and whereas Eli had gone on to law school, Lex had gone to grad school to get his MBA. Lex and his family owned numerous furniture stores in over twelve states across the country.

"What do you mean that some of the older members of the business council are talking about backing Samuel Nesbitt?" Eli asked.

Lex held out his hand. "Calm down, Eli. I'm just the messenger who by right really shouldn't be telling you any of this. I overheard my old man talking on the phone and thought considering our friendship, I'd give you a heads-up."

Lex then dropped down in the chair across from Eli's desk. "From what I gather, they all know you're the most qualified—hands down. You're an astute businessman, a brilliant attorney, and savvy when it comes to knowing the right people and making things happen. But..."

Eli's eyes narrowed even more. "What's the damn but?"

"You have a reputation around town. They see you as a notorious playboy, who likes to dazzle and bed the ladies. They don't know if you're suitable to be president of such a prestigious organization yet. They are looking at someone who's settled down. More focused." Lex chuckled. "Someone who wouldn't be a threat to their daughters."

"This isn't funny, Lex," Eli growled.

"In a way, it is. With all you have going for you and with all the things you can bring to the table if you were to become president, what they're concerned with most is your inability to keep your pants zipped. It's not only amusing, it's downright crazy. And you don't have to be reminded that a few months ago everyone heard about that affair with your secretary that went sour."

Lex shook his head. "Unfortunately, your reputation is under scrutiny by a few of the older men with clout and the ability to influence the others. That's why they have begun making calls trying to get people over to their way of thinking. You know you have me and my dad's votes, and I'm sure you'll get the votes of your own brothers. But I can't speak for anyone else at this point. You have a couple of months to change their opinions of you and I suggest that you do it."

"And how am I supposed to do that?" Eli snarled.

"By doing whatever you can to clean up your playboy image, even if it means getting a wife."

Eli almost fell out of his chair. "A wife! Are you crazy?"

"No. Honestly, that's the only way I think you're going to win them over. A fiancée wouldn't even work for you since they know you have a habit of dumping women when you get bored with them. A wife is the only way you'll win the presidency. You can kiss the office goodbye without a Mrs. Elijah Steele."

Blood rushed to Eli's head. For the past seven years, he'd done all the right things to make himself stand out. Now a bunch of old men still wanted to run things by dictating how he should live his life in order to get the position he rightly deserved?

"You know the younger members were depending on you to take control, Eli. It's about time. Harry Farmer has been president too long and he would love making sure Nesbitt gets the presidency since they have the same conservative views about change. Nesbitt is already married and settled, which is the only advantage he has over you."

And that was an advantage that could cost him the one thing he wanted, Eli thought, building a steeple with his fingers under his chin.

"The presidency can lead to other things for you, Eli. Think about it. President of the Business Council now, mayor of Phoenix later. You know a lot of women. Surely there is one out there who will agree to marry you to move your political aspirations forward. Hell, you're a Steele. Women will clamber all over themselves to marry you."

"No," Eli said in a firm voice thinking of the kind of women something like that would draw.

"No to what? No, there's not a woman you'd want to be shackled with, or no, you're not willing to sacrifice your livelihood for something you really want?"

Eli rubbed his chin as the vision of Stacey Carlson flickered across his mind. He could definitely see himself shackled with her. But then on the other hand, the entire thought of marriage made him want to choke.

"Just think about it. I like coming home to the same

woman every day, Eli. Marriage has its benefits. Hell, you can even make it a marriage of convenience with the right woman. Have her sign a contract for a year or so, just long enough for you to reach all your goals."

Lex stood as he glanced down at his watch. "I need to leave, but I hope you consider all the possibilities, Eli. You owe it to yourself and the future growth of Phoenix to do so."

A short while after Lex left, Eli pushed the document he'd been trying to read aside. His mind was refusing to concentrate. Instead, it wanted to focus on what Lex had said and that idea he'd implanted into Eli's brain.

A wife for hire.

Was there a woman who'd go along with such a thing without getting attached to his name? One who'd willingly give him a divorce when he asked for it without things getting ugly? He was an attorney so he could draw up his own documents, and the legal aspect of it would be so iron-clad a woman would be crazy to do anything but abide by the terms. But to be on the safe side he would seek counsel from a divorce attorney.

But first he had to consider what he had of value to give the woman. Of course, there was the issue of money, which could always be depended on to be a motivating factor.

He frowned when again the image of Stacey Carlson floated through his mind. Quite naturally since she happened to be the last woman he kissed, thoughts of her would be fresh—pretty damn potent—in his mind.

He pushed his chair away from his desk to stand and stretch his legs as he thought some more. First of all, there was the possibility everyone would know his marriage wasn't on the up and up. He'd be able to fool some people, but no one in his family would believe he'd go from staunch bachelor to a happily married man. It had worked that way for Galen but it wouldn't for him.

But if he and the woman were convincing enough, it could work. He rubbed a hand down his face, not believing he was actually considering such a thing. He glanced at his watch. He had to be in court in an hour and the last thing he needed was taking personal matters into the courtroom, especially since Judge Tilly Madison was on the bench. He was convinced on some days the forty-something woman was a man-hater.

Grabbing his jacket off the rack and his briefcase off his desk, he left his office, pausing at his secretary's workstation just long enough to let her know he'd be in court and afterwards he would be grabbing lunch at Easterling's.

He had a lot of thinking to do and he might as well do it on a full stomach.

Stacey glanced down at the menu to study that day's lunch specials. She'd decided to use her lunch hour and get out today instead of rushing through lunch in the backroom of her shop. Besides, it was a beautiful day, the first week of November, and she figured she deserved to be outside enjoying it for at least a little while.

She had talked to Cohen earlier and she could still hear the excitement in his voice. He was working with a realtor in Florida who had found him what he hoped was the perfect place. It was right on the Atlantic Ocean. She couldn't wait to see it and looked forward to her first visit after he got settled in.

She looked away from the menu for a moment and studied the other persons who'd come to this restaurant for lunch. She could tell some were holding business meetings, but most were couples who'd met to enjoy lunch together.

She tried ignoring the huge disappointment that touched her chest when she thought about the number of times she and Wallace had not dined together. They had done so in the beginning, but then he'd found every excuse for them not to go out. She should have recognized the signs then since, according to Dee, he was now wining and dining Gail like nobody's business.

It wasn't easy for a woman when a man lost interest in her. She knew she hadn't been an expert in the bedroom, but still. What happened to the guys who were willing to teach their woman a thing or two instead of expecting them to be all experienced? Although Wallace had never told her she was a disappointment, the mere fact that he hadn't slept with her during the last year they were together spoke volumes.

She was determined the next time she got serious about a man she would know a lot more about what a man enjoyed in the bedroom than she did now. But how was she supposed to learn all that stuff? It wasn't like there was a Lovemaking 101 class being offered anywhere.

Her thoughts shifted back to Wallace and Gail. That she would be running into the couple at Dee's parents' anniversary party in a few weeks was a bitter pill to swallow. But she refused to let the couple steal her joy… even the little joy she did have.

She wouldn't let Eli steal her joy, either. She didn't

have a clue what his problem was and she knew she shouldn't really care. But she did. And for the life of her, she didn't understand why. If a kiss from him could leave her pining, she didn't want to think how things would be if they were to sleep together. It would be best to steer clear of him so she wouldn't have to find out.

As she looked down again at her menu, she felt a presence standing by her table. Thinking it was her waitress coming back to take her order, she glanced up and her gaze collided with a pair of green eyes. So much for thinking she could steer clear of Eli.

Eli had convinced himself when he walked into Easterling's and glanced around and saw Stacey sitting alone at a table, that seeing her again had nothing to do with the increase of his heart rate. Nor did it have anything to do with that quiet fluttering in his chest. But now that he was staring into the deep darkness of her eyes, eyes that reminded him of the sweetest chocolate, he wasn't sure anymore.

He inhaled sharply when she put down the menu she'd been holding against her chest, and revealed a pair of firm breasts that were pressed tight against the blouse she was wearing. Nice. He'd always considered himself a leg man but her breasts had him thinking.

"Eli?"

Her voice all but stroked him, and he continued to hold her stare while trying to hide his intense reactions to her. "Stacey. How are you?" he asked, fighting off the way his heart rate had increased even more. What the hell was wrong with him?

"I'm fine, and you?"

"Great." Eli recognized his response as a lie even before it had left his mouth. He wasn't doing great. He had deliberately avoided her over the past few days. And now there was a campaign going on to knock down his bid as president of the business council. He had every reason to be in a bad mood but found he couldn't. For some reason, seeing her was brightening up his day.

He glanced around and then back at her. "Will someone be joining you for lunch?"

"No."

"Do you mind if I do?" he asked. He could tell by the look on her face, one she quickly tried to hide, that his request surprised her. He understood. He knew it was obvious he had been avoiding her lately so why was he seeking her company now?

"No, I don't mind."

"Thanks." He pulled out a chair and sat down and immediately knew he'd missed her. Hell, he'd missed her a lot. Ever since their kiss, he couldn't get the vision of her naked, her long gorgeous legs spread, waiting for his entry, out of his head. His erection stirred at the thought and he could actually imagine her moaning in his ear. He was certain he would receive the satisfaction of his life, and so would she.

He made a conscious effort to force such erotic thoughts from his mind. Why was it so difficult? Okay, it had been over six months since he'd made love to a woman. Liz had left such a sour taste in his mouth he'd placed a lock on his zipper for the first time in his life. But now, Stacey had him forgetting about how deceitful and manipulative some women could be.

Glancing across the table, he saw she was trying to avoid eye contact with him. "Have you been avoiding me, Stacey?" he asked, looking over at her and wondering if her skin was as soft as it looked and thinking he would love to find out.

She glanced over at him and he saw the fire in her eyes, fire he would just love to quench. "I could be asking you the same thing, Eli."

He couldn't help but smile. God he loved that fire. He also liked the way she'd tilted her head to glare at him and how an errant curl fell in her face. He was tempted to reach out and push it back. He didn't want anything covering her eyes since he liked drowning in their dark depths.

"Well?" she asked in a voice dripping with mild sarcasm as she all but glared at him.

He didn't see any reason to lie to her, so he leaned over the table and in a low tone admitted, "Yes, I've been avoiding you. However, it was either avoid you or seek you out for a repeat performance of what happened between us last week. Only thing, Stacey, I wouldn't stop with just a kiss. I'd go further and take you against those boxes that had excited you that day. And I'd show you what real excitement is truly about."

Stacey tightened her grip on her water glass while every part of her body began to ache. How could mere words from his lips do that when a touch from Wallace hadn't come close to having the same effect?

What was there about Eli that could uncurl such turbulent emotions and desires within her? And why could something as innocent as his scent make her think about things that had no business flowing through her mind? She nervously licked her bottom lip and noticed how his gaze shifted from her eyes to her mouth.

"And I wouldn't do that too many times if I were you. Or I'll be tempted to kiss you here and now. If only you knew just how much I've thought about that tongue of yours lately."

Stacey sat down her glass before it fell out of her hands. The man who before last week had very little to say was now sprouting a mouthful of lustful words that had her quivering inside. Her gaze narrowed. "I dare you to try it."

Eli quirked a brow. Evidently, she didn't know him. Apparently, no one had warned her that he was the one Steele who didn't take dares easily. And the dare she'd placed on the table would not only be a piece of cake, it would be a whopping scoop of vanilla ice cream on top.

"Fine," he said, easing his chair back. "Let's skip lunch and go back to your shop. I'll give you a lunch treat you won't forget. Ever."

He watched her lips tighten and he smiled to himself. She would back down. There was no doubt in his mind that she would. What he'd suggested was outlandish, over the top, too far out there, but he'd meant every word. He waited, prepared for her to tell him just where he could go and how quick to get there. But then suddenly, he sensed something. A shift, a change, an emergence of edginess he knew well. However, it was a state he had a feeling she not only wasn't accustomed to, but one she would find hard to handle.

Intrigued, he couldn't help wondering what she was

thinking. Was it the same thing he was? Would she take him up on his offer? But more important, not that he had any complaints, why she even considering doing so?

Stacey knew she had gone too far with this Steele, but she couldn't help doing so. Maybe she could lay blame on the call she'd received from Dee. Whatever the reason, she felt the need to do something out of the norm for her. And taking up one of Phoenix's most notorious players' suggestion of a quickie for lunch was something she normally wouldn't consider doing in a million years.

So why was she doing so now? Why did the thought of making love to him, having her body connected to his, have her head spinning in desire? And it was desire to a degree she'd only begun experiencing since meeting him.

He was watching her, waiting. What happened to the good girl her aunt Maggie had raised? It didn't take long for her to remember that same good girl had gotten dumped by the man she thought would love her forever.

She looked over her shoulder and knew she had to make up her mind and quick. Their waitress would be returning to take their order at any moment. She blew a curl out of her eyes and returned her gaze to Eli. He was still watching her with an intensity that stirred everything inside of her and she felt herself succumbing even more to his sensual draw. He wasn't saying anything. Instead, he was letting her decide on her own, although she was well aware of his preference.

She began nibbling on her bottom lip and again his

gaze followed her actions. She suddenly stopped when she recalled what he'd said the last time. She also recalled something else. The kiss they'd shared last week and her nightly fantasies since then. They had been naughty fantasies about him before, but the kiss had sparked even more arousing ideas. Ideas she wanted to play out in reality.

She wanted him and had no illusions about love. Love had nothing to do with it. The man she'd once thought of as her Prince Charming had turned into a frog and she was convinced there wasn't another prince out there for her. She wouldn't waste her time waiting; instead, she'd become one of those women who went after what they desired.

She'd never been an aggressive woman when it came to men, but today she wanted to get what she wanted. She took another sip of water and met his gaze. Before she could change her mind she stood and said, "Okay, let's go."

Eli stared at her as he stood as well. He opened his mouth to ask her if she was sure of her decision and quickly shut it. He'd never questioned a woman's decision about making love with him and wasn't about to start now.

But he intended for them to have as much time together as possible. "I suggest we don't go back to your shop. My place is closer."

Chapter 6

Turning his car down the single lane leading to his home, Eli glanced over at the woman sitting beside him. He had suggested they take one car and later he would return her to Easterling's to get her vehicle.

He thought Stacey was like a puzzle with all kinds of pieces he needed to put together to see what he would get in the end. There was no doubt in his mind that she wanted him as much as he wanted her, but he was getting vibes that maybe he needed to slow things down and find out what was really going on in that mind of hers. Initially, he'd convinced himself he didn't give a damn, but honestly, he did. Why, he wasn't sure, but he did.

He looked over at her when he brought the car to a stop after pulling into his driveway. She was wearing a skirt and as his gaze roamed over her he could tell she'd lost some of the brazenness from the restaurant and was now nervous at the prospect of spending intimate time with him. The way she was gnawing on her bottom lip was a sure sign.

Getting out of the car, he made his way to the other side to open the car door for her. The Steele brothers might be sexual hellions, but the one thing Eden Tyson Steele made sure of was that they had manners—although they might not display them all the time.

"Thanks," Stacey said.

"You're welcome."

Other than discussing her brother's move to Florida, they hadn't done much talking on the drive over and that had been deliberate on his part. He had wanted her to really think about the decision she'd made. And there was no doubt in his mind that although she was having some misgivings about her decision, she had made one. Otherwise, she wouldn't be here.

"This is a nice house, Eli."

He smiled as they moved toward his front door, appreciating her compliment. "Thanks."

He was proud of the house he had purchased a few years ago, which gave him a beautiful view of the mountains from his bedroom window each morning. They were the same mountains he used to ride his horse on every Saturday morning after finishing his chores. His parents lived on the other side of that same mountain. Not too close but close enough.

When they reached his front door, he turned to Stacey fully expecting her to tell him she'd changed her mind. But when she merely met his gaze, he was held immobile by the desire he saw in her eyes and suddenly couldn't wait until he got her inside.

Already he could see himself doing a lot of things to her, and the first thing he would do would be to strip her naked. His hand trembled with need when he turned the lock and opened the door. Stepping aside, he let her enter first.

The moment the door closed behind them he didn't waste any time pulling her into his arms, capturing her mouth with his and holding her solidly against him. He loved the feel of her body pressed to his. And when it came to her mouth he was hungry for it, literally starving, and he took it with a greediness that made his stomach ache with a need that was taking control of his senses.

This was the first woman he'd let invade his space in a while and this kiss was definitely making it worth it. The chemistry between them had been strong from the very beginning and now it was nearly burning out of control. It was pure animal lust. And he intended to take advantage of it.

Stacey was making such a thing real easy. Why? And why did he care that she was? Especially considering the fact his erection was throbbing mercilessly and practically dying to get inside of her. Still, he would tell her the same thing he told all the others, to make sure they were on the same page and there wouldn't be any misunderstandings.

He broke off the kiss and whispered against her moist lips. "This has nothing to do with love Stacey, just sex."

She blinked and he watched something akin to regret flash in her gaze. And then she met his eyes and murmured in a low tone, "I know what this is about, Eli.

I'm a big girl. I can handle a casual affair. No emotional entanglements. Trust me, I get it."

He stared at her for a second, certain that she probably did, but…

Eli pushed the "but" to the back of his mind. He had given her every opportunity to change her mind and she hadn't. So he would happily take whatever she offered and run to the nearest bedroom with it. It was the Steele way. But there was something about her entire acceptance of what they were about to do that bothered him. A part of him felt that maybe they should talk about it, but unfortunately, his body wanted to skip any closing arguments.

Instead, his total mind wanted to concentrate on the delectable-looking woman with the long, gorgeous legs standing in front of him. They had wasted enough time and now he was ready for action.

Stacey hadn't known there were so many erogenous spots in the human body. At that very moment she was feeling each and every one of them inside of her come alive. They were actually shivering under the intensity of Eli's gaze.

She was well aware he was having misgivings about sleeping with her and she was bothered by the notion that possibly he hadn't found her attractive enough. Was that the reason Wallace had left her for Gail as well? Gail was perky, vibrant and wouldn't hesitate going after what she wanted. She'd always told Stacey that she thought Wallace was a good catch. Too bad she'd decided to steal Stacey's man. But then he hadn't really been her man. If Wallace had been, he would still be with her and not Gail.

She drew in a deep breath, deciding she didn't want to think about her ex-friend and her ex-fiancé any longer. She wanted to concentrate on the mass of masculinity standing in front of her. She was ready to peel that shirt off his body and touch all the corded muscles beneath. She was ready to do some things with him she'd never done with another man. She felt adventurous.

And now they had less than an hour.

But some things couldn't be rushed and being here with him was her first official declaration of freedom. Eli would be the first man she would share a bed with since Wallace. Dee would be the first to say it was about time.

Even now she could feel the chemistry. It was strong and had been from the first. And there was no doubt in her mind that their coming together would be explosive. At least it would for her and she hoped she wasn't a disappointment to him.

Suddenly, he bent down and brushed a kiss across her lips and whispered, "I can tell you're beginning to think too much."

She smiled. He was right. She was thinking too much. It was time for a little action. She took a step toward him and reached up to place her hands on his shoulders and eased her body closer to his. She tried not to react to the feel of his throbbing erection pressed against her. It was hard to believe he actually wanted her that much. Knowing that he did made her feel desired. Sexy. And it showed her how much her confidence as a woman had taken a beating with Wallace.

She let out a soft shriek when suddenly Eli scooped her up into his arms. He smiled when he glanced down at her and said, "We're taking an extended lunch since we're going to need more than just an hour."

Eli walked through his house with Stacey in his arms liking the feel of her there. To some they were moving too fast, but as far as he was concerned they weren't moving fast enough. They didn't know everything about each other, but he felt they knew enough. After all, this wasn't one of those forever sort of things. He intended to make it as casual as it could get. She'd called it nicely when she'd said *no emotional entanglements*. He didn't do those types of entanglements. In the end they could get messy.

But he had no problem going after pleasure and he was anticipating it with every step he took. Hell, he couldn't wait to get his clothes off and strip her as well.

Entering his bedroom, he swiftly crossed the room and placed her in the center of his bed. He watched as she glanced around and saw the smile that touched her lips when she returned her gaze to his.

"What a spacious bedroom you have, Eli, and this bed is humongous. But nothing beats the view outside the window. It's gorgeous."

"Thanks."

He had the house built a few years ago and he'd paid extra attention to how he wanted his bedroom, making sure he could wake up each morning with the view of the mountains staring him in the face. His bed was a double king and had been custom made by the brother-in-law of his cousin, Sebastian Steele, who lived in North Carolina.

Eli's brothers would often tease him about the number of women he could have in his bed at one time since it was so big. But he wasn't into multiple bed partners. One woman with a lot of fire would do him just fine.

His gaze roamed all over her. The first thing he intended to do was strip her naked and the second was to savor her all over. He was determined to find out if she tasted as good as she looked. And he was known to have a sweet tooth and a ravenous tongue when it came to anything he enjoyed. And he had a feeling he would be adding her to his list.

"Now for your clothes," he said, reaching out to unbutton her blouse while holding her gaze. Moments later, he gently pushed the blouse from her shoulders and smiled at the way her bra was holding her breasts hostage. He could tell by the way they were pressing against the thin material of her bra that the creamy brown twin globes wanted the freedom he intended to give them.

He reached behind her to release the clasp and his erection began throbbing when they spilled out of her bra that he quickly tossed aside. Never had he seen such perfectly made breasts. His stomach clenched when he thought of just how ripe the dark nipples were for his mouth.

"Now for your skirt," he said, and eased back while she shifted her body. He took his time tugging the material down her hips and they were such a curvy pair.

She wasn't wearing a slip and the skimpy panties barely covering her below the waist left a lot to view.

"You might want to remove these yourself or I'm liable to tear them off of you," he warned in a deep, rough voice, as his fingers caressed the silky material.

"You wouldn't dare," she murmured sultrily.

She shouldn't have said that. Without missing a beat he reached down and ripped her panties.

Stacey gasped and scooted back from him.

"And where do you think you're going?" he asked, catching hold of one of those legs he liked so much, and liking the feel of her warm skin beneath his fingers. "That's the second time you dared me today, Stacey, and just in case you haven't figured it out yet, I don't take dares very well."

He could see amusement lurking in the depths of her dark eyes. "You don't?"

His response was given in a slow grin. "No, I don't."

Eli's gaze then roamed up and down her body before returning back to the one leg he still held in his firm grip. He smiled at her ankle bracelet. It did something to enhance the look of her leg, made it appear even sexier. He caught one of his fingers in the thin gold chain and gently rubbed it back and forth against her skin. "Nice."

He picked up on her ultra-soft moan and knew she was getting aroused from him rubbing her leg that way. She hadn't seen anything yet and her response to what he was doing sent shivers all through his body, and caused a throbbing ache in his groin that was so intense, he knew he had to get out of his clothes now or suffer irreparable damage.

"Eli?"

"Hmm?"

"What are you doing to me?"

He held her gaze. "Something called foreplay. At least the start of it, anyway."

"There's more?" she asked.

"Definitely. As much as you can handle," he managed to get out in a thick voice.

Seeing her naked on his bed did something to him and for a moment he felt it had more to do with just assuaging a physical need. He shook off such an absurd thought. The only reason Stacey was here was because of needs—all physical—and it seemed she had them as well as he. That thought had intense heat seeping into his bones, and he suddenly felt his erection get even harder.

When it came to Eli, Stacey wasn't sure just how much she could handle. His mere touch on her leg was making it difficult to catch her breath. The pads of his long fingers were evoking arousal unlike anything she'd ever felt.

And then he left her ankles and his fingers traced slowly upward toward her thighs, caressing the muscles in her legs as he went. She'd never had a man pay so much attention to her legs before. And his warm hands on her sent shivers racing all through her body and sharpened her senses.

He was staring at her and the look in his eyes was filled with passion and the promise of things yet to come. The thought of her lying there naked for him should have embarrassed her but it didn't. Instead, for the first time in her adult life she felt empowered as a woman.

"I could stand here and look at you this way all day," he said, releasing her leg. "I'm a man who appreciates beauty and you have the most gorgeous pair of legs that I've ever seen." His words stroked her all over, caressing her skin like a feather duster, and the voice saying them was as hot as the pads of his fingers on her skin.

Sensations stirred within her and as she watched, he slowly began removing his own clothes. She almost bolstered enough courage to tell him she would do it, then decided she much preferred stretching out on the bed to enjoy the strip show.

First off was the jacket that he carelessly tossed aside. Next was the Forzieri dress shirt which exposed what Stacey thought was the sexiest chest any man could possess. It was muscular, rock hard, hairy. As her gaze traveled lower she could see his erection pressing tightly against the zipper of his pants and immediately knew what that meant. He wanted her in a *big* way.

The thought that she could do that to him, or any man, to bring him to such an aroused state touched something deep within her. And it was a part of her that wanted to experience everything with him.

"Now for my slacks," he said, reclaiming her attention. She drew in a deep breath, almost too overly anxious to watch this part. He would be exposing himself, and a part of her couldn't wait. She inched closer, making sure she had a good view.

He smiled, evidently reading her thoughts. "I won't disappoint you, Stacey."

Never for one minute did she think that he would. It

amazed her how in just a little time, after one hell of a kiss, he could go from grunting his words to seducing her with them. From the first time she'd met him and further observed him, she'd gotten the feeling he was a perfectionist and there was no doubt in her mind that fetish would extend to his lovemaking.

And she could pretty much guarantee he was experienced with women. With his reputation she didn't have to wonder. Bottom line, the man was hot, he was lethal and she had a feeling before it was all over, he would set her on fire.

His hands went to his zipper and she followed the movement with a tight breath. The hands that were lowering his zipper were strong, knowledgeable. And when, moments later, he eased his pants down his legs leaving his body confined in a pair of black briefs, she released a moan.

And when he inched those briefs down his thighs she thought she would pass out. The man was so well-endowed she automatically licked her lips in deep appreciation. She could only stare, take it all in, every impressive inch of him. The head of his penis was huge, hard and so powerfully male she could feel her body ache. And she could feel her body doing something else as well. She was getting wet, right there in her center just from looking at him and wondering how he planned to use that part of his body on her. And he would. She was certain about that.

Then as she continued to watch, he pulled out a drawer to his nightstand, reached inside and took out a condom, which he proceeded to put on. He glanced up, met her gaze. His mouth curled into a sexy smile, and then he was moving, coming back toward the bed and she knew she was about to experience passion to a degree she'd never known before.

Chapter 7

He had to have her. Now.

Eli had planned to draw it out, ply her with foreplay of the most intense kind. But after seeing her lying on his bed in such a tempting position while watching him prepare himself for her, he couldn't wait any longer.

And she was lying there waiting, as calm as she pleased, when she probably ought to be running down the stairs and out the door as fast as those gorgeous legs could carry her. He'd never wanted a woman to this degree before and wasn't sure to what extent his control would last.

He didn't want to rush things but he intended to show her the real meaning of excitement even if it killed him. He would make sure she got her pleasure many times over before he would even attempt to get his. He stopped walking when his knee touched the bed.

"Come here."

His breath lodged in his chest as he watched her ease up in a fluid movement and inch toward him. When she was close enough, he reached out and gently hooked a hand behind her neck to bring her mouth closer to his. Then he lowered his own and kissed her the way he'd wanted to do that other day. He was devouring her, leaving no inch untouched. In putting everything he had into it, he was getting affected by the kiss as well. This kiss was deep and it was touching a place inside of him no other kiss had visited.

Then he broke off the kiss, leaned in toward her chest and caught a nipple into his mouth. He smiled at the way it easily slid between his lips. He tugged on it, sucked it deeply, laved it with his tongue then sucked on it some more. He heard her moan, felt the sound in every part of his body and it nearly made him come then and there. But this wasn't about him. He intended to make it all about her.

Moments later he pulled his mouth away and eased her backward onto the bed. He leaned over and lifted her leg to his lips and began kissing it, working his way from her toes up toward her center. His tongue was licking and laving its way up her leg and enjoying the taste of her smooth skin along the way.

She had tilted her head up to look at him. He knew how she was feeling by the way her breath was being forced in and out of her lungs. And her dark eyes were glazed with a degree of desire that was affecting his mind. It was desire that he reciprocated in every part of his body.

He couldn't stop the fire from blazing in his loins when the path his mouth was taking led him straight to the juncture of her thighs. He paused long enough to breathe in her scent and without wasting any more time, he lowered his head between her legs and went straight to her feminine core.

"Eli…"

Her husky moan was almost lost on him, the sound quickly smothered by the deep thump in his chest. He went about tasting her with a greed he hadn't known he had, with a ravenous hunger that was gripping him, pushing him over the edge in such a way he couldn't help but taste her to his fill.

And then he felt her body explode beneath his mouth. He felt her thighs tremble and then she screamed his name. *His name.* And the sound charged the air, entrenched him in something he'd never felt before.

He quickly moved his mouth away from her to shift his body upward and straddle her. When he was there, settled between her open legs, he studied the look in her eyes, the heated gaze that was staring back at him as she tried getting her breathing under control.

"Make love to me, Eli," she whispered in a choppy voice.

"I plan to." And he meant it. He intended to ride her hard. She had awakened feelings, stirred them to life, in a way no other woman had before. He needed to get back in control and hoped those lingering fantasies of making love to her—the ones that kept him up at night, that had him going into her store during the day making purchases he didn't need—would finally be put to rest. He was certain it was curiosity of the unknown that was driving him to act so out of character with a woman. Especially this woman.

Once his hips were just where he wanted them to be, cradled within her thighs, he glanced down at her again. As their gazes locked he began easing his body into hers. The connection made his entire body tremble.

She was tight and her inner muscles clamped down on him. Sucking in sharply, he sank farther and farther into her wetness. He gritted his teeth and found even that wasn't working against the intense sensations erupting inside of him. "Hell."

He buried himself into her to the hilt, then he reached out and gripped her hair and began moving, riding her like his very life depended on doing so. Her muscles clamped him tighter as he thrust into her, rocking back and forth and going even deeper still.

"Eli!"

Then it happened again for her. He felt the way she exploded, literally came apart beneath him. Her tremors passed through to him, pushing him to increase his thrusts, stroking her into a third climax. And when her hips bucked up at an angle that clenched his shaft, while wrapping those gorgeous legs around him, he knew it would be the closest he'd ever get to heaven. Eli could only accept that together they were taking the art of making love to a whole other level. He loved the feel of being inside of her. It was simply incredible. He felt overwhelmed, overcome in passion so thick that when he grinded his hips against her again, his entire body exploded. He came in one torrential release, riding her in a way he'd never ridden a woman and with the strength and reckless abandon that had his pulse throbbing in his temple.

"Stacey!"

He shouted her name and threw his head back as lights seemed to flash before his eyes. A kaleidoscope of radiant colors blinded him, prolonged his orgasm while white-hot heat rushed through him, ripped into his muscles and sank like sharp teeth into every inch of his skin.

No woman had ever done that to him, threw him into such an intense climax while her muscles continued to clinch him, virtually milk him dry. He felt heaven. He felt like a man on top of the world, on top of the most sensual woman to ever walk on the face of the planet.

The scent of her was assailing him at every angle and he continued to make love to her with a primitive hunger that wouldn't let up until he lost control once again, exploding inside of her like he'd never done before.

Moments later when he felt his body go limp, he eased off her, rolling onto his side. Not ready to let her go, he reached out and pulled her closer into his arms. At that moment nothing mattered, not even the fact he probably would be late for his four o'clock appointment today.

"I enjoyed making love with you," he murmured close to her ear and realized just how much he actually meant it. He had enjoyed it too damn much. He closed his eyes, drew in a deep breath. And at that very moment he knew he was in a world of trouble.

"We need to talk, Stacey."

Stacey inhaled deeply before glancing over at Eli. He was still stretched out on the bed naked. They had dozed off after making love, and after awakening, she'd quickly begun dressing with all intentions of calling a cab and leaving before he woke up. But now with him wide awake there was no way to carry out her plan.

She tugged her blouse into her skirt while slipping her feet into her sandals. "Maybe some other time, Eli. I hadn't planned to be away from the shop this long. And I—"

"No, Stacey, we need to talk."

Stacey stared at him. He hadn't raised his voice one iota, but he'd spoken with a steely edge that demanded consideration. Was he one of those men who stated how things would be both before and after a toss between the sheets? If he was concerned she had not fully understood how things were between them the first time, then he had nothing to worry about. She knew the sex had meant nothing to him, although it had meant everything to her. It had proven she was a woman with feelings and emotions. A woman whom a man could find desirable. A woman who, thanks to Eli, had discovered her passionate side.

Fully dressed, she turned to him and tried keeping her gaze leveled on his face and not on his body, which wasn't an easy thing to do considering he was aroused again. She couldn't help feeling a quivering in her belly when she took note of that.

"We've talked already and nothing's changed. You have nothing to worry about," she said, hoping that would ease his mind.

Annoyance flared in the depths of his green eyes. "That's not what I wanted to discuss."

If that wasn't it, then what was? Another possibility crossed her mind. Was he having regrets because she leased space in a building he owned and that was too close for his comfort? Did he assume she would deliberately get underfoot? Become possessive? She knew about his last girlfriend from a conversation she'd overheard between Cohen and Tyson.

She squared her shoulders. "I am not the clingy type, Eli," she said, hoping she had assured him of that.

She watched as in a graceful fluid movement, he eased from the bed and spotting his briefs on floor, picked them up and slid into them. It was then that he crossed the room to her. He reached for her hand and lightly traced a thumb over her wrist. She felt herself shiver beneath his touch and knew he'd felt it as well.

"I never thought you were," he said, lifting her hand to his lips and brushing a kiss across her fingers. "But I need to know what this day was about for you," he said in a low, husky tone. "You can't convince me spending your lunch hour in a man's bed is normal behavior for you."

She lifted an arched brow. "But it could be for you?"

He smiled. "Yes."

She shouldn't be surprised. But what he'd said was true. It was not normal behavior for her and she might as well be honest with him about it. "I've never done anything like this in my life."

He nodded as he lowered her hand but he didn't relinquish it. "Then why did you do it today?"

The answer to that was easy, although she wasn't sure she would share it with him. She had wanted him from the first, had been curious about him, had entertained numerous late night and early morning fantasies about him. But she probably would not have acted on either if she hadn't received that call from Dee.

"I got a phone call before I left for lunch," she heard herself say. "From my best friend back in Memphis."

When she paused too long to his way of thinking, he took a step closer. "And?"

And I truly wish you'd put on some clothes, she started to say but clamped her mouth down from doing so. Although she would be the first to admit to enjoying the view, there was something about an almost naked man who had a body that could make a woman drool. And when it didn't take much to recall the sexual expertise of that man, that made matters even worse.

With the slightest pressure on her hand, he regained her attention. "Stacey?"

He was saying her name in that ultra-sexy way of his. A tone that would tempt anyone to spill her guts about anything he wanted to know, and she felt herself yielding to that temptation. "Dee's parents are celebrating their fortieth wedding anniversary the week after Thanksgiving. I've been invited."

She knew her explanation didn't make any sense and he proved her right when he asked, "So you felt driven to make love to me because your best friend's parents are celebrating an anniversary?"

She fought back the urge to tell him she hadn't actually been driven to make love to him. It was something she had wanted to do for some time; she just figured she never would.

"There's more to it than that, Eli," she said.

"Lord, I hope so."

His words, spoken in a sexy breath, nearly weakened

her at the knees and she pulled her hands from his, took a step back and eased down in the winged-back chair in the room.

"I had promised Dee I would attend the party months ago, not thinking that Wallace would probably be there."

"Wallace?"

She tilted her head up to look at him. "My ex-fiancé. And of course he would be bringing Gail."

"Gail?"

"Yes, the woman he dumped me for. So I guess you can say I decided to have a pity party."

"Because you haven't gotten over him?"

He had picked his shirt off the floor and was putting it back on. She watched how easily it slid over his broad shoulders and how his fingers—those fingers that had touched her practically everywhere just moments earlier—were now buttoning up his shirt.

"Oh, I've gotten over him, trust me," she finally responded. "I just don't like being reminded of being played. Gail was my friend. At least I'd thought she was."

She didn't say anything for a minute and then she chuckled. "Dee thought of a plan for me to get back at both of them, while at the same time regain a little female pride."

"And what plan is that?" he asked, slipping into his slacks. He had thick sinewy thighs. They were tight, muscular and she could vividly recall her legs wrapped around them while he thrust in and out of her body. She had been filled with an all-consuming need and he had taken care of it in the most delicious and mind-boggling way.

"Stacey?"

"Yes?"

"What was your friend's plan?"

She met his gaze. "She suggested that I return to Memphis with a boyfriend, or better yet, a pretend fiancé in tow, just to prove I haven't been pining for Wallace, and to show that no matter what they did, I dusted myself off and kept right on living."

There, she'd told him. He was the only person she'd shared Dee's plan with. "Does that sound silly or what?" she asked, smiling. Sharing Dee's idea with someone else made her realize just how ridiculous it was.

"It doesn't sound any sillier than an idea my best friend gave me today," Eli said, shaking his head while sitting on the edge of the bed to put on his shoes and socks. "He thinks I should consider getting a wife for hire."

Stacey raised a brow. "Why would you want to do something like that?"

"Trust me, I don't," he said, his words sounding like a harsh grumble in his throat. "But as crazy as it sounds, I might have to."

She shifted in the chair and tucked her legs beneath her. "But why?"

"I want to be president of Phoenix's Business Council. It's an elite group that I've been a member of for years. It's time for the group to be led in a different direction—one with vision—and as president, I plan to do that."

He stood and grabbed his jacket. "Only, a lot of the older members with clout don't see me as a viable candidate because of my reputation with the ladies."

Stacey frowned. "What does that have to do with your ability to be the leader they need?"

"Nothing, but they are making it an issue. They want a president who's settled down. A married man. If I didn't want the presidency so bad, I would tell them all to go to hell. But in this case, I can't do that."

She shook her head. And she thought that she had problems. She didn't say anything for a minute and then she smiled over at him. "The one thing we have in common is that we have best friends who can come up with some crazy ideas."

"Yes, I'd have to agree with you on that."

She stood when she saw he'd finished dressing. He glanced at his watch. "I'll make it back to the office in time for my four o'clock appointment," he said. He looked over at her. "You have a little more than an hour before closing time."

"Wednesdays are usually my slow days," she said, glancing around, trying to recall where she'd put her purse. "And I plan to finish unloading all those holiday decorations."

He didn't say anything and she slowly held her breath when he walked toward her. He was fully dressed and she could admit to thoroughly enjoying the opportunity to having seen Eli Steele wearing nothing at all.

Eli came to a stop directly in front of Stacey. She looked good. She smelled good. And she was good. He doubted he would ever forget the feel of her legs wrapped tightly around him or the way her inner muscles had clamped down on him while he'd thrust back and forth inside of her.

And then there was the way her tongue had tasted when he'd made love to her mouth. Their tongues had dueled in a kiss that he wished could have lasted forever. He had come hard, harder than he'd ever come inside a woman before. He had felt it. His orgasms had been intense. Unforgettable. Each thrust inside her body had prepared him for the next…and the next.

"I enjoyed making love to you today, Stacey," he said, remembering how her screaming his name had been incredibly erotic.

"And I enjoyed making love to you as well. It was quite an experience."

That made him smile. "Excitement of a different kind?" he asked.

She returned his smile. "Most definitely."

He paused a moment, glanced down at the floor and then back at her. Although they'd enjoyed today and he would admit it was the best lovemaking he'd ever experienced, he knew from here on out he would have to keep his hands off her. What Jonas said last week was true. If Cohen left Stacey in Tyson's care, his brother would be difficult; especially if he found out Eli was sniffing behind her.

"Today was all there can and will ever be between us," he said in a low voice tinged with regret.

"I know."

He hadn't expected her to be so agreeable. "You're okay with that?"

"Yes. Why wouldn't I be? I told you what happened

today wasn't normal behavior for me. In fact, this is the first time I've made love in more than a year."

He lifted a brow. "More than a year? But I thought you broke up with your fiancé around seven months ago."

"I did. But he suggested we stop making love way before then. He claimed he wanted to make our wedding night that much more special." She frowned. "The real reason he hadn't wanted to make love to me was that he preferred banging around with Gail instead."

He heard the bitterness in her voice and a part of him wondered if perhaps she was still carrying a torch for this Wallace guy, although she'd denied it earlier. "I can't imagine a man not wanting to make love to you, Stacey. Like I said earlier, you were great."

He reached out and gently cuffed her chin, forced her to look at him. "I felt things I hadn't felt before." He saw the skeptical look in her eyes and said, "And I'm not running a game on you, or telling you what I think you want to hear. You were better than in my dreams."

"Dreams?"

He chuckled. "Yes. I've had several dreams of having sex with you, but the real thing is better than a dream any day." There was no need to tell her that from the first time he'd seen her at Cohen's birthday party, she had turned him on like nobody's business and in a way no other woman had ever done.

"I like everything about you," he said in a voice so deep he barely recognized it as his own. He then leaned close and swiped the tip of his tongue across her lips. "And I definitely like the way you taste."

And then he kissed her, taking the fullness of her

mouth in one sensual sweep. And while his tongue took control of hers, devouring her mouth, he reached up to run his fingers through the curls on her head. Stacey could bring out needs in him quicker than any woman he knew. It was a good thing they were both on the same page as to not wanting a repeat of today. But damn, he enjoyed kissing her. And he didn't want to think about making love to her.

He slowly pulled his mouth away and licked his lips afterwards. His erection was throbbing again. If he didn't get the hell out of there he would be stripping her clothes off again. And that wasn't good, especially after they'd decided today was it for them.

He took a step back. "Ready for me to take you back to the restaurant to get your car?"

"Yes."

"Okay then," he said. "Let's go."

Chapter 8

Stacey scanned her gaze over the guest list. Cohen said he wanted a small party that only consisted of his closest friends. She chuckled thinking her brother had more close friends than he realized. There were those who worked with him at the hospital, the guys he played golf with on Wednesdays and, of course, the Steeles. Everyone was told they could bring a date and she couldn't help wondering if Eli would jump at the chance to do so.

It had been almost a week since she'd seen him. Exactly one hundred and fifty-three hours since she had slept with him, made love with him and shared back-to-back orgasms with him. She'd heard he'd had an unexpected trip out of town, but that was a couple days ago. What happened to the days in between?

Stacey tossed the guest list aside thinking she really didn't have to ask what had happened to those missing days. They had agreed their one time was the last. Her hormones had gotten the best of her that day and his testosterone had bombarded him. It happened. They had dealt with it. They'd since moved on.

And now she was dealing with this—a feeling of withdrawal. Of intense need from a long-denied addiction. And it wasn't for just any man. It was for him. Eli Steele. But it had been a mutual agreement there would not be a repeat performance.

The bell on her door chimed letting her know she had a customer. Her heart began racing when she glanced to her right and saw the tall, dark-haired handsome man, and then she quickly sucked in a disappointing breath when she recognized Eli's brother, Mercury.

Mercury Steele was almost two years younger than Eli, but just like with Eli's other brothers, you could tell the men were related. Those green eyes and dimpled smiles were a dead giveaway. And speaking of their dimpled smiles, he had one on his face as he strolled over to the counter.

"Hi, Stacey, I'm glad you haven't taken all your Halloween stuff down yet. Does that mean you still have a few items in stock?"

"Yes, in fact we're having an After Halloween sale. I thought it would help to reduce inventory."

"Good. A couple of the guys I represent were out of town playing football on Halloween and didn't get to take their kids trick-or-treating. I thought I would host a private Halloween party in my home."

Stacey nodded, thinking doing something like that was thoughtful of him. She knew Mercury—a former NFL star himself before an injury shortened his career—was sports agent to several well-known football and basketball players. "Come on. Let me show you what I still have."

A few moments later she was ringing up all of Mercury's purchases.

"I'm surprised you still have some of these left," Mercury said, indicating the bag of candy corns. "Eli always had a weakness for them. He must not know you had any."

She shrugged as she bagged his purchase. The mere mention of Eli's name started her stomach quivering. "I'm not sure."

"But then the reason could be because he's been out of town for the past week and—"

She glanced back up. "He's been out of town for a full week?"

"Just about. It was supposed to be a two-day business trip, but something came up and he had to extend that time."

Stacey didn't say anything as she ran his credit card through the system. She'd known about Eli's two-day trip since his secretary had mentioned it when she'd come in to make a purchase. But she hadn't known he'd eventually been gone all week.

"I heard about the party you're giving Cohen."

She glanced up at Mercury thinking how much he favored Eli. "Yes, and you will definitely get an invitation. And you can bring a date."

"No, thanks. Women tend to get clingy when you take them to a party. They all but want to stamp ownership on you. Not worth the trouble to bring one. I'll have more fun going solo."

She wondered if all the single Steeles felt that way. And for the second time that day, she wondered if Eli would be bringing someone.

Eli glanced at his watch as he walked off the airplane to head toward baggage claim. A part of him was mentally drained. He'd figured he would be gone for two days but instead he'd been away for seven. The trial had taken a nasty turn when one of the former employees of the company he represented claimed Eli's client had deliberately withheld safety information putting their employees at risk.

It had been hard reclaiming the upper hand to paint a picture of a corporation that cared about its employees after that, but he had and had eventually won the lawsuit. But in a private meeting afterward with the top brass at Byars, he had threatened to walk if the company didn't make changes in its safety policies. He didn't have the time or the inclination to represent any company that didn't play by the right rules and whose mismanagement could endanger the lives of its employees. In the end, he was certain the people at Byars understood him loud and clear.

Grabbing his luggage, he walked out of the airport and headed for the car he'd left parked in the garage. The only calm to his hectic week had come from nights remembering that one day he'd spent with Stacey. Hell, it hadn't even been a full day, just a few stolen hours in his bedroom. But the time had been both productive and effective because he had enjoyed the best sex of his life.

And that's all it had been, he convinced himself

as he moved toward his car. He and Stacey had both agreed to throw out emotional entanglements that day and that's what he preferred. Emotional entanglements could be messy and it was the one thing he would not tolerate in his life.

Why was he even thinking about it? As far as he was concerned, sleeping with Stacey that one time was one of those "one and done" things. He'd been intensely attracted to her, had needed to get her out of his system, especially after their kiss, and making love to her had been the solution. So why did the thought of making love to her trigger a hunger within him? A craving that was invading every bone in his body, converging on every cell?

After tossing his luggage into the trunk, he opened his car door and slid onto the seat. It was a dusty hot day, unusual for this time of the year, and he would kill for a cold beer about now. His thoughts shifted back to Stacey and the day they had spent those hours together. He had actually fallen asleep with her sleeping beside him in his bed. When was the last time he had slept during the day and done so with a woman cradled in his arms?

Although he'd hated being gone for a week, in a way, he'd needed that time to put distance between them. When she had told him about her friend's suggestion about taking a pretend fiancé to Memphis with her, he had come close to volunteering for the job.

And what had enticed him to share Lex's conversation with her? Probably because she had told him of her best friend's outlandish suggestion, he'd felt comfortable in doing likewise. Eli tried to switch his thoughts to other things but couldn't. The image of Stacey and how she'd looked that day, beautiful and naked in his bed, came tumbling back to the forefront of his mind each and every time.

When he brought his car to a traffic light, he reached up and loosened his tie. The thought of Stacey was making him simmer inside. What the hell was wrong with him? It wasn't like he hadn't slept with beautiful and desirable women before. He had, countless times. And he couldn't help racking his brain trying to determine what had been different. Why was Stacey Carlson so embedded into his thoughts?

And why had he missed her like crazy?

Before he could talk himself out of it, he switched his car's blinker on and pulled to the side of the road. Tugging his iPhone from his pocket, he strolled through his list of contacts to find Stacey's gift shop. One of the requirements of all his tenants was to provide him with emergency numbers in case they needed to be contacted. His pulse began thumping wildly when he pressed her home number. It was Saturday evening. She might not be home. Probably had a date.

"Hello."

He wouldn't ask himself why relief swept through him when she picked up the phone. "Hello, Stacey, this is Eli."

"Eli?"

He could tell she was somewhat surprised to hear from him. It was on the tip of his tongue to say, yes, this is Eli. The man who you slept with a little over a week ago. The man who gave you three orgasms back-to-back, and who would have loved to have given you a fourth. The man who can't seem to get you out of his mind.

And the man who would give just about anything to make love to you again.

"Yes, this is Eli. Did I catch you at a bad time?"

"No. I just got home a few moments ago. I'd been out shopping."

"Umm, buy anything?"

"Yes, mostly makeup."

He wondered why she bothered. Her skin would probably look good without it. "I'm just returning from Chicago. In fact, I haven't made it home from the airport yet and was wondering..."

"Wondering what?"

"If I can drop by and see you."

She paused on her end, and he could imagine her nibbling on her bottom lip with her teeth. Then she said, "Yes. If you want to."

"I do. We can go out somewhere if you'd like." What he really wanted to do was take her to the nearest bedroom and jump her bones, pump inside of her real good more than a few times. He was getting hard just thinking about it.

"Are you sure you want to do that? Go out, I mean. You just got back to town and you're probably tired."

A look of disappointment crossed his face. Was she hinting at the possibility that she didn't want him to come over, or go out with him? "So would you rather I not drop by, Stacey?"

"I don't know, Eli. Can you give me one good reason why you'd want to?"

He could give her more than just one good reason.

But since that's all she had asked for... "I missed you," he said simply. It was the truth. He had never admitted such a thing to any woman because he'd never missed any woman before.

She didn't say anything for a moment and then, "In that case, yes, you can drop by because I missed you, too."

A smile touched Eli's lips. Hell, why was he smiling? Why did the thought that she missed him make him feel good? Vibrant? Hornier? "Give me your address and I'll be there in a few."

When he clicked off the phone he was still smiling.

Stacey placed her cell phone back by her bedside. There was no doubt in her mind why Eli was dropping by. She couldn't help wondering what had happened to their "one and only time together" agreement?

Maybe she should not have admitted to missing him. But when he had openly admitted to missing her, she had weakened. The one good thing was that she knew where she stood with him. Unlike with Wallace there would not be any false illusions. Eli was a man who was up-front with women. He didn't lead them on. He was not a man who'd ever commit to any one woman and that was what she needed since she would never commit to any man again. She refused to get emotionally involved with one. She had learned her lesson. Eli's heart was just as off-limits as hers and that was a good thing. She wouldn't want it any other way.

As she left her bedroom to head downstairs, an idea popped into her head. He'd mentioned he had just returned home and was on his way from the airport. That meant he hadn't had a chance to unwind yet. She smiled when she thought of the bottle of wine that one of her regular customers had given her this week, and figured now was as good a time as any to open it.

A short while later, she heard the doorbell just as she finished setting the bottle of wine and the two glasses on her kitchen table. She had a small kitchen and the drawn curtains gave the room an intimate effect.

She couldn't help the butterflies that flapped in her stomach at the thought that Eli had actually come here. She looked down at herself. The first thing she'd done after returning from shopping was to hop into the shower. With no plans to go back out today she had changed into a short caftan in a vibrant floral print that provided a somewhat exotic flare. She enjoyed wearing caftans during her downtime and thought they provided the ultimate in relaxing comfort.

She inhaled deeply as she moved toward the door and in her mind she detected his scent even before opening the door. It was robust, definitely male and it sent everything female inside of her reeling in anticipation of seeing him again. It had been a whole week.

With her heart beating like crazy in her chest, she glanced out the peephole just seconds before turning the knob and opening the door. And there he was. Eli Steele.

He stood there, in her doorway, his green eyes sharp, smoldering and sensual. He was staring at her like he was the big, bad wolf and she was Little Red Riding Hood and within seconds he planned to gobble her up.

She felt every muscle in her stomach quiver, tighten in response to that look, and without saying a single word, she slowly began backing up. He responded to her retreat by advancing toward her, taking time to close the door behind him, but continuing toward her with a stealthy, slow and furtive move that had her pulse racing.

And when he came to a full stop in front of her, her eyes locked with his and the heat, the need, the hunger, reflected in the green depths made the juncture of her thighs tremble and she could actually feel her panties get wet.

She felt breathless. Her nipples were painfully erect and pressing against the material of her caftan. A deep shudder passed through her and she could feel it all in her clitoris. It was beginning to throb, awaken with a life of its own. Whenever she thought of that day they'd spent together in his bed, she would sum it up in her mind as reckless impulse. In that case, what would you call this?

She dragged in a deep breath and said, "No emotional entanglements." As if Eli needed to hear that as well, have it reinforced in the recesses of his mind. She watched his eyes darken even more, saw them become filled with even more desire.

He then repeated what she'd said. "No emotional entanglements."

And then she watched as he took a single step back to shed his suit jacket, remove the already loosened tie from around his neck and toss both on her recliner. His white shirt was tucked neatly inside his pants but soon he began tugging it out, unbuttoning it. She could only stand there and stare, watch and get aroused by the second. When he was through undoing his shirt, he peeled it off and then stood there, bare-chested and showing strong, muscular shoulders and a flat tummy dusted with black hair that led a path past his waistline to be hidden by his pants.

"I thought about you every single night, Stacey," he said, kicking off his shoes and bending to remove his socks.

His words seemed to echo in the quiet stillness of the room, the sound ricocheting off the walls. The timbre of his voice caused goose bumps to form on her arms and she slowly found herself losing a grip on reality. Instead, she was oozing into fantasy land and the man standing before her had always occupied a place there.

"But do you know what I thought about most of all?" he asked as he straightened and began undoing the belt to his pants.

She watched the motion of his hands, felt a hard lump in her throat, and saw the hard erection pressed against his zipper. She forced herself to speak. "No, what did you think about most of all?"

"Being inside of you. Remember how your body took me in then held me hostage, clenching me tight, drawing everything out of me."

His words painted a picture she could vividly remember and could still feel. Which was probably the reason her clitoris continued to throb something awful. "Why are you telling me that?" she asked in a voice she could barely hear herself.

"Because I need you to understand my hunger, but more important, my need for you."

And she saw that need as he lowered his slacks. She

tried to retain her composure but even the hardwood floor felt hot beneath her bare feet.

"I want to make love to you. Here. Now. All over this living room. Then later we'll make it to your bedroom. What do you think about that, Stacey?"

She swallowed, barely able to think at all. She tried shifting her thoughts onto the wine she had waiting for them in her kitchen, but couldn't. They could drink some later. Afterward. But right now all she could think about was the man standing there, in the middle of her living room, wearing a pair of briefs with an erection the size of which should probably be outlawed. He wanted her. She detected his desire in his features, his breathing and especially in the way he looked at her.

"Stacey?"

"Yes?"

"You didn't answer. I asked what you thought of me making love to you all over the place."

Remembering what he'd once warned her, she forced her gaze up from his huge erection to look into his eyes and said, "I dare you."

Chapter 9

Eli never considered himself a slow person, but he hadn't known just how fast he could move until he'd crossed the room and pulled Stacey into his arms. He began devouring her mouth with a greed he felt in every cell of his body. Every single molecule.

The moment his tongue reunited with hers he felt her reaction, and it drove him to taste her even more. She tasted hot. She tasted delicious. Kissing her, entwining his tongue with hers, was giving him unparalleled pleasure.

But he wanted more.

He broke off their kiss and in an instant he had removed the short, sexy getup she was wearing and began touching her all over. She didn't have on a bra and those barely-there undies didn't count. When he had her completely naked he stood there and began stroking her skin, leaving no part of her untouched. He enjoyed the way her nipples responded to his touch and the way her inner muscles tightened around his finger when he reached down and inserted it inside of her.

"Why are you doing this to me, Eli? Why do you enjoy torturing me so?" she asked in a heated rush when he bent his head to capture a nipple in his mouth and suck it. She ran her fingers over his head and the feel of her touch sent flashes of arousal through him that magnified at the head of his erection.

He needed to get inside of her now.

Eli moved to lower his briefs down his legs and when he straightened, she reached out and in an unexpected move she took hold of his shaft. He threw his head back thinking how warm her hand felt on him and then when she began roaming her fingers all over him, stroking him, his moan of pleasure reverberated throughout her entire room.

"How does that feel, Eli?"

He had to inhale a few times before he could speak. "So damn good."

"And how does this feel?" she asked, moving her naked body closer and keeping a tight grip on his erection as she rubbed it over her belly and thighs. He was throbbing mercilessly against every part of her that his shaft touched. When she shifted her body and opened her legs it was there, poised at her entrance. Ready. "And just so you know, I'm in good health and on the pill," she met his gaze and said.

"I'm in good health as well," he eased through tortured lips.

"Good. Then do you want to come in for a visit?"

she leaned over and asked close to his ear, taking a lick in the process.

Hell, he wanted to do more than just visit. He intended to make himself at home. By the time he left she would surely think he had worn out his welcome.

Instead of answering her, he quickly reached out and hoisted her off her feet, spread her legs and thrust inside of her. He felt her legs wrap around him as he made it to the nearest wall, which was only a few feet away.

The minute her back pressed against it, he couldn't wait and began moving. He kept a tight grip on her thighs as he went in and out of her. Pressure began building in his belly with every hard thrust. They were skin to skin and he couldn't recall the last time he'd made love this way. Maybe never. Pill or no pill he never had sex with a woman without using a condom, so what the hell was he doing, screwing her against the wall unprotected?

He determined the answer moments later when she screamed his name. And as if on automatic pilot, he felt the first spurts of release leave his body and travel into hers. She was giving him pleasure of the most intense kind and his body was reciprocating, holding nothing back, even the semen he'd guarded all these years like his life depended on it. But he was giving it to her, shooting her right into another orgasm and enjoying every single moment of doing so.

"Stacey!"

He went after her mouth, captured it in his and gave her a tongue-tingling kiss he didn't ever want her to forget. He definitely knew that he wouldn't. Every nerve in his body was on fire, and as he continued to kiss her and make love to her, his body felt even more energized. And then he felt it. He was coming again. Heaven help him! When was it going to end? He figured no time soon as long as her gorgeous legs were open and wrapped around him tight. His shaft was still throbbing inside of her, even while bursting in yet another release.

Incredible.

Stacey quietly eased out of bed and glanced back over her shoulder at the man sleeping there. A smile touched her lips. They had started out making love in the living room and at some point ended up in here. When, she wasn't sure. She wasn't even sure how they'd done it after refusing to separate their bodies even for a second. She had never done anything like that in her life with a man. Certainly not with Wallace or that guy she'd slept with that one time in college. Neither man had had a lasting effect on her where sex was concerned and neither man could hold a candle to Eli. He was male sexuality on two legs both going and coming.

And speaking of coming…he had the stamina of a bull and the longevity of a sitcom that refused to go off the air. He was awesome. She grabbed her bathrobe off the back of the chair and slid it over her naked body while thinking Eli Steele had a way of making a woman feel sexy and desired. Not all men could do that. Wallace certainly never had. She figured she needed to stop comparing the two men since there was no comparison. Eli had no equal. Even Wallace would realize that if he and Eli ever met, which wouldn't happen. She could just imagine Wallace sizing him up and knowing he'd failed miserably in contrast.

She tried to push thoughts of Wallace out of her mind, and instead, as she headed down the stairs, her thoughts went to the one person she did want to think about. The man she'd left sleeping in her bed.

There was no such thing as getting enough where he was concerned, but the intensity of his desire didn't bother her. Especially when he could stimulate her like nobody's business. If he got his then he made certain she got hers. He had to be the most unselfish lover.

Totally exhausted from making love, they had dozed off to sleep. She had awakened later to find his head resting on her belly and didn't have to recall how and why it had been there. She smiled at the memory and later, after he practically made a meal of her, they had dozed back off to sleep again.

When she'd awakened this last time, his erection—still somewhat hard although he was sleeping—was nuzzled against her backside as they slept in the spoon position with one of his legs thrown over hers. When she had untangled from his hold and eased out of bed, he had flopped on his back and continued to sleep.

When she reached the bottom stair she gazed around the living room. Usually she was a tidy person, but clothes—both hers and his—were strewn everywhere. She was glad Cohen, who would usually drop by unannounced, was working the night shift at the hospital. She could imagine what his reaction would be to find she had a Steele in her bed. He, more than anyone, knew how the Steele men operated and the thought that his sister had gotten tangled up with one, intimately so, would have sent his blood pressure boiling.

Although Cohen knew she was old enough to make her own decisions, he still had that protective instinct where she was concerned. He'd never liked Wallace and hadn't hesitated to let her know it. He liked Eli well enough, considered him a good friend and would probably continue to do so as long as he didn't know Eli was sharing his sister's bed.

When she made it to the kitchen, she paused. Although she and Eli had made love on two different occasions, he was not sharing her bed. At least not on a frequent basis. Tonight would probably be the last time he dropped by. Why he wanted to do so now was a mystery, just like him saying he'd missed her.

She looked at the bottle of wine on the table as well as the two glasses. They would probably have a drink together before he left. She glanced over at the clock on the stove wondering when that would be. It was close to midnight and he seemed to be sleeping rather peacefully. She didn't have the heart to wake him.

She glanced over at the book she had begun reading last night and decided since she wasn't sleepy, she could stretch out on the sofa and continue reading. When Eli woke up and noticed her gone he could come looking for her if he wanted her.

And she had a feeling that he would.

Eli slowly opened his eyes and glanced around the room. Pink. He blinked and sure enough the predominant color in the room was pink. He was certain he'd noticed it when he'd carried Stacey in here. But then he might not have since his mouth had been locked to hers the entire time and his concentration had been on her and not his surroundings.

He shifted his position in bed and her scent from the bed linens consumed him, tantalized him in the way only her aroma could. Nice fragrance. He closed his eyes then quickly opened them. What the hell was going on here? What was happening to him? He glanced at his watch and saw it was close to one in the morning.

Hell! When was the last time he'd felt this comfortable in a woman's bed? Okay, he would admit that for four hours he'd had the hottest sex of his life, and he meant hot with a capital *H*. But that was no reason for his mind to start acting crazy on him. And the last thing he needed was to let his guard down.

And he'd made love to her without a condom. It hadn't been an accident. He'd known full well what he was doing. But he had wanted her and had wanted to feel her in a way he'd never felt another woman. Why?

He didn't have to think hard about that one. Things with Stacey were different. He couldn't explain why yet but he knew they were. But he didn't want things to be different. He was Eli Steele and he wasn't prone to succumb to any woman, no matter how good she was in the bedroom.

What he needed to do was get the hell out of there so he could think straight. That hot, enticing scent of hers was affecting his brain and his ability to think. He pulled himself up in bed and glanced around. When he didn't see his clothes, he remembered where he'd left them. Downstairs. He had gotten out of his clothes after less than five minutes of being inside her house.

Naked, he padded his way to the door. He had no qualms walking through her house naked and hoped when she saw him that she didn't have any complaints.

When he got downstairs to her living room he glanced around. He didn't see her but heard soft music coming from her kitchen. He noticed his clothes had been picked up off the floor and were neatly placed on her table. Moments later, he had slipped into his briefs and slacks when the smell of onions and green pepper stimulated his nostrils and stirred his stomach.

Shirtless and barefoot, he opened the kitchen door and his heart nearly stopped beating. And his groin began throbbing into an erection the size of New York. Stacey was bending over, looking in her refrigerator for heaven knows what, and presenting him with an eyeful of the sexiest bare backside he'd ever seen. He tamped down his thoughts of how he would like to get her from behind.

He drew in a deep breath forcing his body not to cross the room and do just that. He glanced around her kitchen and saw the bottle of wine and wineglasses. He leaned against the door and said in a voice that sounded husky for even his ears, "That short robe isn't covering much, Stacey, and what I'm seeing is something I definitely would like to have."

Stacey swirled around, nearly dropping the water bottle out of her hand. She drew in a deep breath and stared across the room at Eli. And then she wished she hadn't. He was leaning against her kitchen door with that just-barely-awake look on his face, in a stance that had sexy written all over it.

His face appeared smoldered in passion and those green eyes were ablaze with desire so thick you could probably use it to butter your bread. How could a man who'd made love to a woman for four hours straight, take a nap and wake up with a look that all but said he wanted to roll between the sheets again?

For a moment she couldn't move and couldn't even speak. She just stood there and stared. He had slid on his pants and she wondered how, after being tossed on the floor, the slacks had retained their sharp crease. There wasn't a wrinkle in them anywhere. And some men, she thought, had chests that were made to be shirtless and his was one of them.

Knowing she needed to say something instead of standing there staring like a nitwit, she said, "Sorry, the flash wasn't intended."

She closed the refrigerator door and leaned against it. "I thought you'd be sleeping for a while. In fact, I had tried lying on the sofa and reading but my concentration kept getting interrupted."

He lifted a brow. "By what?"

"Your phone. It kept ringing. Someone is trying to find you."

He shrugged. "Probably one of my brothers."

She smiled. "Probably."

"Maybe I need to explain things."

She shook her head. "No, you don't owe me any explanations."

"I don't?"

"No. Remember our agreement. No emotional entanglements. Although we've made love on two occasions, we aren't officially lovers. Besides, I knew what you were before making love to you."

He continued to stare across the room at her and she felt the heat from his gaze. "And what am I?"

She wished he wouldn't look at her like that. Like he would love to taste her all over again. "You're Eli Steele. A man who enjoys women."

She noticed he didn't deny her claim. "And you don't have a problem with that?" he asked.

"Heavens no. I would only have a problem with it when it pertains to my health. And you've assured me you're healthy and I believe you. You don't come across as a man who would take risks."

"I don't."

"Then I don't have anything to worry about. Now, would you like to share a glass of wine before you leave?"

Chapter 10

She was kicking him out?

Forget about the fact that less than ten minutes ago he'd made plans to leave on his own anyway, it was the principle of the thing. And the principle, according to the book of Eli, was that he always decided when he left a woman's place. No female had ever suggested it was time for him to go. Usually, they begged him to stay.

A barely-there smile touched his lips. "You want me to leave?"

"Why would you want to stay?"

Oh, he could give her countless reasons. Pass him a piece of paper so he could make a list. At the top would be the fact that although they weren't officially lovers, like she'd just said, he'd shared a lot more of himself with her than he had with any other female. Pill or no pill, good health or not, he had made love to her without a condom, releasing his semen inside of her plenty of times over.

He rubbed his hands down his face. Never had he been confused about a woman. Maybe she was right. He should share a glass of wine with her and split.

"Hey, you okay?"

He glanced over at her. "Yes. Let's share the wine and then I'll be out of your hair."

"No rush."

You could have fooled me. "I'll finish dressing."

He left the kitchen and walked back to the living room. As he slid his shirt over his shoulders, he thought that maybe he ought to take a rain check on that wine since it seemed she wanted him gone. Maybe the sooner the better for her.

"You're pouting."

He paused buttoning his shirt to glance over at her. He narrowed his gaze. "I wouldn't know how to pout, Stacey," he said matter-of-factly.

A smile touched her lips as she leaned back against the breakfast bar that separated the living room from the dining-room area. He wished he didn't know she was naked underneath that robe. And he sure as hell wished she wasn't standing in a position that showed her long, gorgeous legs that way.

"Could have fooled me, Eli. You're doing a good job of it. And not to offend your sensibilities, I'd love for you to stay the night, but the reason you have to leave is because Cohen is working the night shift. And usually when he does, he drops in for breakfast unannounced on Saturday mornings. I don't think it will be a good idea for him to find you here in my bed."

Eli paused. He hadn't considered that possibility and she was right. He liked Cohen, but her brother had been friends with the Steele brothers long enough to know how they operated and would kill any one of them he thought was taking advantage of his sister. Stacey was an adult but all that wouldn't matter to Cohen.

Eli tucked his shirt into his pants. "Then I need to thank you for making sure we don't encounter unnecessary drama."

"You're welcome, and I'd love for you to share a glass of wine with me before you left. Honestly," she said. He then watched as she turned and sashayed back into the kitchen.

Stacey couldn't help but smile. Eli had been pouting because he thought she was dismissing him like he'd probably dismissed a number of women over the years. And he had looked so cute with his kissable lips sulking. What was really cute was that he hadn't been aware he was doing it.

She glanced up when he walked into the kitchen looking like the Eli Steele she knew, all neat as a pin in his designer duds. "I've already poured you a glass."

He sat down at the table across from her. He picked up the glass, studied the contents for a while before glancing back at her. "You and Cohen are close."

She nodded. "Yes. And it's going to be hard when he leaves for Florida."

He took a sip of wine and then said, "I'm surprised he didn't persuade you to go with him."

She chuckled. "Trust me, he tried but like I told him, I have a life here."

"But no man to share it with?"

She leaned back in her chair. "No. I'm in no hurry. I tried believing in the forever-after thing and it didn't work. Now I believe in reality and not fairy tales."

He shook his head. "Don't get cynical. Your guy was an ass as well as an idiot. You're better off without him. Eventually you'll dust yourself off and get back into the game. Marriage suits a woman like you."

A woman like her? "How do you figure that?"

He shrugged. "I can't explain it but I know. Sorry your ex damaged your beliefs about something like that."

She was intrigued. "You're a fine one to talk. You and your brothers are womanizers, yet your parents, from what I understand, have a very happy marriage. Can you explain that?"

He stared down at his wine for a moment and then looked back at her. "Easily. We take after my father who used to chase women before he married my mother."

He chuckled. "He even got run out of Charlotte in his younger days."

Stacey's eyes widened. "You're kidding, right?"

Eli chuckled. "I kid you not. He had so many fathers and mothers gunning for him that his cousins had to slip him out of town one night. Even now whenever he returns to visit, it's done very quietly."

Stacey studied his face and saw he was dead serious. "But he eventually put aside those despicable ways after meeting and falling in love with your mother."

"Yes, and you've seen my mother so I'm sure his decision was understandable and pretty damn smart." Eli continued to bask in amusement when he added, "And as you know, Galen met and fell in love with Brittany, which is also understandable."

He paused briefly, took a sip of his wine and then said, "I'm sure it will happen to the rest of us one of these days. At least according to my mother it will. But the remaining five of us are banking on it happening later rather than sooner. We're having too much fun."

"Yeah, I bet."

He didn't say anything for a moment, but sat there staring into his wine while absently twirling the glass between his fingers. Then he glanced up at her. "I enjoyed making love to you tonight, Stacey. You're amazing."

A shiver ran down her spine with his compliment. He had said pretty much that very same thing the last time, and she wondered if he told that to all his women. "And I enjoyed making love to you, too. I think you're amazing."

The room got quiet as they sipped their wines each lost in their own individual thoughts. She tried to fight it but on occasion they would look over at each other. It was during those times that she could feel the sexual tension building between them again. It was stroking her skin like an intimate caress.

He glanced at his watch, slowly stood and said, "It's almost two in the morning. I better go."

She stood as well. "Okay. I'll walk you to the door."

Stacey circled around the table and when she was close to him, he reached out and gently pulled her into his arms. He leaned in closer, pressed her body close to his and lowered his mouth to hers. She felt a rush of heated desire the moment he kissed her. In seconds he began devouring her mouth with a hunger that she actually felt in every part of her body. And when he took hold of her tongue, feasting on it with intense greed, she felt weak in the knees.

He then ended the kiss with the same energetic force with which he'd begun it. Then he reached out and pushed a curl back from her face before leaning back down to brush a kiss across her lips. "I wish I could say this was the last time for us, Stacey, but I have a feeling it's not."

She nervously licked her lips. She had a feeling it wasn't the last time, too.

Chapter 11

"Eli, are you listening to anything we've said?"

Eli blinked at his brothers, remembering they were even there. They had shown up at his place a few moments ago claiming they'd been worried. They'd known he had returned to town and couldn't understand why he hadn't answered their calls.

"I heard you," he all but said in a snarl. "The four of you assumed someone had done me bodily harm."

His youngest brother Gannon's eyes narrowed. "Not just anyone. We were worried that you got gobbled up by that crazy woman you hired as your secretary last year. She's a stalker and we heard she's back in town."

Eli raised his eyes heavenward. Gannon had the ability to get theatrical at times. But still, Eli hadn't heard Liz was back. However, he wasn't worried since he'd threatened to slap a restraining order on her ever since she'd made a scene when he'd been on a date with another woman, and had threatened to do horrible things to certain body parts of his. "Well, now you all know that wasn't the case, so you can all go home and get into your beds so I can get into mine."

"We're having breakfast with Galen and Brittany. Besides, it's eight in the morning on a Saturday. What were you doing all night?" his brother Mercury asked, taking a sip of the coffee he'd helped himself to making.

As far as Eli telling them what he'd been doing all night, his lips were sealed, especially since Tyson was one of those waiting on an answer. "None of your business," Eli all but growled.

Gannon laughed. "That could only mean one thing."

"We thought Liz had left a bad taste in your mouth where women are concerned," Jonas added, rubbing his chin as if he was trying to figure out something. "Evidently, some woman has come along and caught your eye."

The woman had done more than caught his eye. She was holding it pretty damn steady…among other things. Instead of responding to Jonas's statement, Eli said, "Look, guys. I know you all missed me last week, but I really need my sleep. I just got in around three this morning," he said without thinking, and regretted the slip the moment the words had left his mouth.

"How come? Your flight got in around seven."

He glared at his youngest brother. Eli had to remind himself that with five older brothers and barely out of his twenties, Gannon was still going through growing pains. He felt just about anything his brothers did required scrutiny. Especially if it involved a woman. For some reason, Gannon assumed they were super humans in their sexual escapades.

"None of your business," Eli said, although he knew being elusive would only give Gannon more ideas.

"So you've given up on the idea of running for president of the business council," Tyson said, as a way to change subjects. It was a move Eli appreciated, although he wished for a different topic of conversation.

"No, I haven't given up anything."

Jonas chuckled. "You might as well. I heard Nesbitt has it in the bag."

"You heard wrong. Nesbitt doesn't have what it takes to run the council. That position is mine."

"Well, good luck. He has Farmer's backing."

Eli ran his hands over his face. He'd heard it all before from Lex. "Don't lose any sleep over it. I will be the business council's next president." Eli made the statement with a degree of confidence that he refused to let be eroded, regardless of Farmer's decision not to back him.

A few hours later, after his brothers had left, he slid back between his sheets, wishing they were Stacey's sheets instead. Hers had smelled good. They'd smelled like her. He wished he was still in her bed. Wallowing in her sheets. Her scent. And still firmly planted inside of her, between those gorgeous legs.

He flipped on his back and stared up at the ceiling. What was he thinking? Why was he obsessing over one particular woman? And now that he'd made love to her, he wasn't sure he could get enough of her. It was as if he'd become addicted and that wasn't good.

What was he supposed to do to rectify the situation?

He had tried avoiding her and that hadn't worked. It had only made things worse when he had seen her again. Then he figured once he'd made love to her that would work her out of his system. That hadn't worked, either. Now it seemed she was even more ingrained into the assembly of his brain waves. He went to sleep thinking of her and he woke up thinking of her. Even now his heart rate was speeding up remembering their goodbye kiss.

She had walked him to the door and instead of giving her a peck on the cheek like he'd intended, he'd given her a blown-out kiss that could have led them straight back into her bedroom. The scent of her had driven him to deepen the kiss, and the way his erection had nestled between her thighs had nearly driven him crazy. He had come close to losing it and coming then and there, which was something that had never happened to him before. No woman had ever made him come close to losing control like she had.

And that, he acknowledged once again, was the crux of his problem. He didn't like being that vulnerable. He would have to come up with a plan before seeing her again when he returned to the office on Monday.

Stacey entered her shop, turned off the store's alarm, turned on the lights and eagerly glanced around, releasing a breathless giggle. It was as if she had stepped right into a holiday wonderland. Thanks to Stan Rollins, the building's electrical technician who'd given up his Sunday afternoon, the special lighting from the colorful bulbs overhead shone down on the holiday display, placing emphasis on the decorations.

With nothing to do after church yesterday, she had come here and decorated her shop. By the time she'd finished, it was close to ten at night, but she had been more than satisfied with her hard work. And now, as she glanced around, she knew her customers would be pleased with the results as well.

She had decided to go with the holiday wonderland theme because it highlighted all her glittering Christmas ornaments. The only thing she hadn't done was put up the Christmas tree. She preferred having a live one which meant she would have to wait a few weeks before they went on sale.

She didn't want to think how lonely her Christmas would be this year. At least she'd had Wallace's company last year...or at least she'd assumed she had. Now she knew why he'd cut short the time he'd spent with her, claiming he hadn't been feeling well. She never suspected there had been a reason for him to turn down her offer to go home with him and nurse him back to health.

Refusing to let Wallace's deceit get next to herself, she shifted her thoughts back to Cohen. Just as she'd warned Eli, her brother had popped up at her apartment early Saturday morning, coming straight to her place from the hospital. Since he prepared breakfast, she couldn't complain too much. However, when she kept yawning through the meal he'd asked why she hadn't gotten a good night's sleep. Instead of answering him, she had quickly changed the subject.

After Cohen had left she had gotten back in bed and had slept past noon. She had hung in doing laundry. Later that night she had spoken to Dee. Luckily, her best friend hadn't brought up her suggestion from the other day. And she figured the less Dee knew about her intimate romps with Eli, the better.

She would eventually get around to telling her one of these days but didn't intend for it to be anytime soon. What would she say? *Hey, Dee, the girl who used to swear she would never engage in casual sex has now become a bedroom playgirl for the likes of one of those infamous Steele brothers. Probably the biggest womanizer of them all.*

And speaking of Eli Steele… She glanced over at the clock. It was only a little past eight, and she couldn't help wondering now that he was back in town if he would drop in this morning as usual. She had less than an hour to find out.

She was dusting off the countertop when the tinkling of the bell alerted her she had a customer. Too late she remembered that in her excitement to see her decorated shop she hadn't locked the door behind her.

Her gaze moved toward the entrance and collided with that of Eli.

Eli stood there wondering why hadn't he been able to keep looking straight ahead when he passed Stacey's shop. He had seen her car in the parking lot, so he'd known she was there. He could have taken the back entrance, so why hadn't he? Why was he a glutton for punishment where she was concerned? And why was his heart now thumping out of control in his chest?

He had walked into what appeared to be a Christmas wonderland. The holiday scenery was spectacular, simply breathtaking. But nothing, he thought, was more breathtaking than the woman standing across the room. And what about this yearning he felt, so intense that he couldn't help the urge to cover the distance separating them and take her here and now? It would be the most satisfying quickie he'd ever experienced. He was more than convinced of it.

He tried controlling his thoughts by glancing around at the decorated shop. There were shiny ornaments and garland; snowflakes that actually seemed to be falling from the sky; toy soldiers and Christmas candles. His mother was big on decorating for the holidays but he had to admit, the atmosphere Stacey had created in her shop was unparalleled.

"Eli, you're early."

Had she been so sure he'd show up this morning and had been expecting him? "Am I?"

"Yes. You came for your copy of the *Wall Street Journal* like always, right?"

Even from a distance he could pick up her scent, a luscious jasmine mixed with her own succulent fragrance, and both were bewitching his senses. He hadn't a clue what she was wearing since she was standing behind the counter. Regardless, they had at least thirty minutes and he planned on taking all of it.

Knowing she was waiting for his response he said, "No, that's not what I came for." He quickly turned and locked the door before moving in her direction.

Stacey lost her grip on the dust towel as her gaze held Eli's. He was moving slowly toward her with a sense of purpose and with a look on his face that said she was his target. Their gazes held and the silent thoughts that communicated between them were understood.

He hadn't come just for the *Wall Street Journal.* She drew in a deep breath and wished she hadn't taken in some of his robust scent with it. She knew she had the ability to put a stop to this here and now. She could speak up and say that two encounters with him had been enough. Her confidence was no longer taking a beating thanks to him and his ability to make a woman feel as if she was the most desired and sensual being on earth.

But the nearer he got to her, the more she could concentrate only on those green eyes staring at her...and how much she wanted, needed, to entwine her tongue with his again, to feel the hardness of his muscles beneath his designer suit jacket.

And, if time allowed, to feel the hardness of him inside of her.

She moved from behind the counter and met him in the center of the store. "I suggest we discuss things further in my office, Eli," she said in a breathless tone.

"Lead the way."

And she did so, on wobbly legs and with inner thighs that were clenching against an intense throb between them. She could hear his footsteps behind her and knew he was right on her tail. Literally.

She opened the door to her office and when he followed her inside and closed it behind them, she turned around. And before he could open his mouth to say anything, she reached up, grabbed the lapels of his jacket and brought his mouth down to meet hers.

* * *

Mercy, Eli thought. She was hot. He could feel it in her kiss as her tongue blazed a trail inside his mouth before capturing his own tongue, holding it hostage and sucking on it in a way that nearly brought him to his knees.

Not to be outdone by any woman, let alone by any kiss, he quickly took control, deepened the kiss and then showed her what a real kiss was all about. But he didn't stop there.

She was wearing a dress and with agile fingers and ready hands, he lifted her dress up to the waist while slowly walking her backward. He'd never been in her office before, but all offices had a desk and hers had to be somewhere. He knew he'd found it when she couldn't go backward anymore.

That's when he grabbed hold of her hips and lifted her up and placed her on the desk while widening her legs to stand between them. He broke off the kiss and his hands quickly went to his zipper.

"Let me," she said, brushing his hands away.

It didn't take her any time to get what she was after and the moment she had him in her hands, gripping her fingers around him, he threw his head back to growl in heated pleasure. He didn't recall anything much after that until he felt the head of his shaft being placed right there at her wet entrance. Not able to hold back from something so tempting, he moved forward, thrusting hard and deep inside of her.

"Oh, hell." He thrust hard again. Then again. And when he felt her legs tighten around his waist, locking him in, his control snapped. He kept thrusting inside of her, seemingly going deeper and deeper with each sensuous movement.

He tilted his head, studied her expression and saw the intense pleasure he was giving her with every stroke. He became mesmerized. The passion was undisguised, genuine and as heated as it could get. And he knew the look on his face probably mirrored hers. Only difference, he would throw openly possessive in the mix. At that moment he couldn't imagine any other man making love to her this way. He refused to even consider it.

When she began screaming his name, he quickly bent low to capture her mouth. And then he soared with her, his body shattering hard in one soul-tantalizing orgasm. He kept coming and coming and coming. And her body took and took and took.

He continued to kiss her as he was dragged farther and farther into the aftermath of the most sensuous and delicious quickie he'd ever known.

Chapter 12

It's only lust, Eli tried telling himself later that day, while standing at the window in his office and staring at downtown Phoenix. Nothing was holding his attention—not the fact that it was a beautiful day and he could see beyond Phoenix's tall buildings to the mountains, or the numerous women in the fitness center that was directly across the street. Come to think of it, he hadn't checked out the fitness center in months. At least not since Stacey had opened her shop in his building.

Stacey.

He rubbed his hands down his face and felt his erection throb as it always did whenever he thought about her. That's why he was sure it was only lust. Hell, what else could it be for him to be this obsessed over a woman where he would seek her out before nine in the morning for a quickie? Somehow his mind had convinced him the moment he'd walked into her shop that he needed a part of her to make his day complete. And by the time he'd walked out of her shop, he'd been consumed with a burst of energy he would not have gotten from a vitamin pill or one of those energy drinks. It had come from Stacey. Even now he was anxious to make love to her again. And he didn't want anything quick about it. He wanted to go slow and savor each and every hard thrust.

The sound of the buzzer on his desk got his attention, and he crossed the room. "Yes, Ms. Larson?"

"Your brother is here to see you."

Eli rolled his eyes. "Which one?"

"Galen."

Eli frowned. "I don't recall seeing his name in my appointment book. Did he have one?" He wondered why he was wasting his time asking when he knew the answer.

"No."

"Then tell him I'm busy."

There was a pause. "He said he doesn't care and will wait."

Eli's frown deepened. "Send him in."

It didn't take long for Steele brother number one to walk in, all smiles. The last time Galen had walked into his office smiling and Eli had asked him what the hell he had to smile about, Galen had answered, "My wife." His brother had gone on to say that getting married was the best thing to happen to him. Evidently, he was still feeling that way.

Eli hoped there was a valid reason Galen had dropped by and not just to waste his time with foolishness. Inwardly, Eli was proud of Galen, who'd made his first million while still in college when Galen and his two roommates created video games that became a hit on campus. The three formed a million dollar company for which Eli was the attorney. That was the good thing. The only bad thing was that millionaire or not, Galen had way too much free time on his hands and didn't know the meaning of structure since he'd never worked a nine-to-five job.

The only saving grace was that being married was keeping Galen busy somewhat. When he wasn't in his garage tinkering with the next video game he planned to put on the market, he was helping his wife out by doing odds and ends at the Phoenix office of Etiquette Matters, the nationally known company that Brittany owned.

"What do you want Galen? I'm busy," Eli said shortly, sitting behind his huge desk.

Galen grinned. "Boy, aren't we in a bad mood. When was the last time you got laid, Eli?"

Thoughts of Stacey spread out on her desk with him pumping into her flashed through his mind. He felt a deep stirring in his gut from the memory. "None of your damn business. Now, what do you want?"

"Just checking on you. You've been missing in action a lot lately," Galen said, dropping down in the chair across from Eli.

"I've been out of town."

"Yes, but you came back this weekend. Brittany invited everyone to breakfast Saturday morning and all Drew's sons were present but you. Gannon claims you had a late night."

"And if I did?"

"Nothing. In fact, I think it's great that you're back in the saddle. I was worried after what Liz Baker tried doing, that you were sidelined for life. It's good to know that you've dusted yourself off and you're back to riding again. No pun intended."

Eli narrowed his gaze. It was on the tip of his tongue to tell his oldest brother to watch his mouth. When Galen or anyone referred to his sexual escapades, they seemed to be cheapening the times he made love with Stacey and in his book, there was nothing cheap and sleazy about it.

He leaned back in his chair and studied his brother and then tapped his fingers against his lips a few times. Before getting married, Galen's sexual exploits were worse than any of them. In other words, of the six, Galen was considered the one who was really *bad* news. Once he'd almost gotten run out of Phoenix the same way Drew had gotten run out of Charlotte. In fact, for a portion of his sophomore year in high school, he had been in Charlotte. Drew had to send him to live with their cousins there for a while. That was after Tess Jones, the principal's daughter, had been caught under the bleachers with Galen with her panties down. Mr. Jones hadn't liked that one iota and had kicked Galen out of school for the rest of the year.

"I need to ask you something, Galen, and I need you to give me a straight answer. No bullshitting."

Galen lifted a brow and then said. "Okay."

Eli paused a moment and then leaned forward to ask, "Have you ever met a woman who you were so attracted to you couldn't think straight? You dreamed about her at night and then had naughty fantasies of her in the mornings? And you foolishly believed your day couldn't start, you couldn't function, until you had a piece of her? And that she could make you feel better than anything you thought possible in the bedroom? And you can't wait to see her again? To be with her again?"

Galen held his gaze and nodded slowly. "Yes, I used to be involved with such a woman."

Eli rushed out a relieved breath. Good, maybe he wasn't losing his mind after all. "What happened? What did you do?"

A huge smile touched Galen's lips. "I married her."

It was a beautiful day and Stacey had decided to get out and walk during her lunch hour. She loved downtown Phoenix with its museums, performing art centers and historical sights. The sidewalks were crowded with a lot of people going to and fro. She noticed other shop owners had begun decorating for Christmas and the more she saw, the more she was put in a festive mood.

Now if only she could put into perspective her involvement with Eli Steele. Just thinking about what happened between them that morning sent luscious chills through her body. She had never considered herself a passionate woman until now. Thanks to the workings of Eli Steele she had morphed into someone she didn't know at times.

The old Stacey Carlson would never have gotten physically involved with a man without the promise of everlasting love. But now that she knew such a thing didn't exist, she had no qualms about having a good time with the likes of Eli. He had opened her to a world she hadn't known existed until now.

And all without any emotional entanglements.

She was being introduced to pleasures and passion beyond her wildest dreams, and could only blush when she recalled what happened in her office this morning. He hadn't dropped in a little before noon as usual, and she was glad since she needed the reprieve to think things through.

In all honesty, she didn't see anything wrong with what they were doing. Eli was being Eli, the womanizer, and like she'd told him, what he did with his extra time was his business as long as it didn't affect his health and hers. She was a grown woman and didn't mind being his flavor for the hour since he was definitely hers. They had been up-front and honest with each other from the start so neither was operating on any false illusions. It was about sex and nothing more. She could deal with that. She wanted to deal with it because she was enjoying him so much.

And she didn't have a problem being secretive about their affair. For one, Cohen wouldn't understand and would be totally against her involvement with him. Fortunate for her in that aspect, Cohen would only be in the city less than a week. After the party she would be giving him on Saturday night, he would be leaving for Florida.

She had mailed out the invitations and Eli was on the guest list. Around each other they had the tendency to draw heat. She hoped no one else noticed that heat or how intense it was. And if they did...oh, well.

Stacey glanced down at her watch. It was time to

head back to her shop. She was about to turn around when a holiday display in the window of an exclusive jewelry store caught her attention. There among the holiday decorations was a small Christmas tree adorned with sparkling gold ornaments and sitting on a blue tree skirt. Sitting beneath the decorated tree was a red box that was opened to showcase a beautiful diamond ring. Both the decorations and the ring nearly took her breath away.

She moved closer and all but pressed her nose to the glass to get a closer look at the diamond. She wasn't surprised to see it was a Zion creation. Jewelry by Zion was the rave since Zion was the First Lady's personal jeweler. Stacey bet the ring cost a pretty penny and could just imagine the woman who would wake up on Christmas morning to find such a rock underneath her tree. That would definitely be one lucky lady. Stacey wished it was her and laughed as she stepped back to move on. That was one wish she knew would never come true.

Eli signed off on the last document as he glanced up at the clock on the wall in his office. It was time to end his workday and he knew just where he was headed. He would go home, shower and then pay a visit to Stacey.

He smiled when he thought of her and then frowned when he recalled his conversation with Galen. Eli would never forget that day when Galen had announced to his five brothers that he had fallen in love with a woman they hadn't met. A woman he had known less than a week. For a die-hard womanizer to make such a claim had been unthinkable.

But unthinkable as it might have seemed, Eli had been the one who had convinced Galen to tell Brittany how he felt before she could leave town and be lost to him forever. And he would be the first to say that Galen and Brittany made a beautiful couple and he knew without a doubt they were very much in love.

He sighed deeply as he thought about what Galen had said earlier that day and tried to force the conversation to the back of his mind. The last thing Eli had wanted to hear from his brother was that his love for Brittany had started from pure lust. And it was lust that had eventually transformed into love. He was happy for his brother but knew the same thing wouldn't happen to him. He was smart enough not to get lust and love confused.

He stood and walked across the room to grab his jacket when the buzzer on his desk sounded. He frowned wondering what his secretary wanted. He went back to his desk to find out. "Yes, Ms. Larson?"

"Mr. Farmer is here to see you, Mr. Steele."

Eli raised a brow and a smile touched his lips. Evidently, Harry Farmer had finally come to his senses and realized he was the best man for the presidency and wanted Eli to know he was pulling his support from Nesbitt and was backing him instead.

Suddenly feeling good, downright ecstatic about the older man's visit, Eli slid into his jacket and said, "By all means please send him in."

A few moments later, Harry Farmer walked in with an air of arrogance that Eli had always admired. Harry had made his millions as a young man in the retail business and owned a slew of retail stores all over the

United States, but the corporate office was in Phoenix. The man's loyalty to the city could not be questioned, but what could be was his reluctance to accept change. Some of Farmer's recent ideas for Phoenix's growth did not embrace a city that could become even more of a mover and shaker than it already was. Farmer lacked the very thing Eli had. Vision.

No one had been happier than Eli last year when Farmer announced that he would not seek another term as president of the business council, ending a near twenty-year term. Farmer wanted to spend more time with his grandkids and Eli could appreciate that.

"Mr. Farmer, this is a pleasant surprise," he said, smiling brightly when Ms. Larson escorted the man into his office.

"Eli, I know it's late but I felt the two of us should talk."

Eli nodded. "Good idea. Please have a seat."

The man sat in the guest chair and Eli sat behind his desk. "I think I know the reason you're here, Mr. Farmer."

The man's bushy brows lifted. "You do?"

"Yes, and I totally agree with your way of thinking."

Surprise flirted across the man's face. "You do?"

"Why, of course. I figured sooner or later you would reach the conclusion that I am the right man for the presidency. The only man."

Harry Farmer stared at him for a minute and then shook his head. "Sorry, Eli. That's not why I'm here."

Now it was Eli who looked surprised. "It's not?"

"No, and I regret you assumed that."

Eli regretted it as well. As an attorney he should have

known better than to assume anything. "Then I must ask the nature of your visit," he said, trying to keep his tone void of the disappointment he felt. He'd jumped the gun. Evidently, Farmer had sought him out for legal advice and nothing more.

Harry Farmer leaned forward in his chair and pinned Eli with his direct stare. "I'm here to ask you to drop out of the race."

Chapter 13

Eli kept his mouth from dropping open as he stared at the man. "You want me to drop out of the race for president of the Phoenix Business Council?" he said in a stunned tone.

"Yes."

"But why?" Eli asked, also leaning forward in his chair.

"For the betterment of the council. Don't get me wrong, Eli. I think you'd make a fine president and you'd have Phoenix's best interest at heart. But I don't see you as someone who is ready to lead the council since you're not focused."

Eli frowned. "I'm not focused?"

"No. Although you may argue one has nothing to do with the other, I disagree. It seems you spend most of your time and efforts pursuing women and I really don't know how dedicated and effective you'd be in the role of president."

Eli drew in a deep breath and fought back the temptation to tell Farmer to go to hell and take his opinions with him. But he of all people knew the weight the man carried within the council. Just like he knew it would be a waste of time trying to convince Farmer just how wrong his opinions of him were. As far as Eli was concerned, when it came to multitasking he was at the top of his game. He could run the council and still pursue women even with his eyes closed.

His mind began spinning and he had to think quickly. The one position he'd always wanted within the community, the one that could eventually propel the political career he intended to have, was slowly slipping away from him. He refused to let that happen.

"Is your only reason for not backing me as president that you consider me a notorious playboy and not settled and focused?"

"Yes. Even with all my conservative views, I would admit your ideas for leading Phoenix forward are good, even better than Nesbitt's. But, unfortunately, several of us can't get beyond your dating history."

Eli nodded. And unfortunately, because of the weight the man carried, Eli needed his support. Knowing he was about to tell a little white lie, one he hoped wouldn't come back and bite him on the ass, Eli said smoothly, "I'm glad to hear you say that because other than my family, no one knows what I'm about to tell you and I hope you can keep a secret."

The older man looked intrigued. "Of course I can keep a secret. What is it?"

Eli once again considered the benefits of the lie he was about to tell. It was hard to believe he was about to fix his lips to say such a thing, but he had to do something. Drastic times called for drastic measures and quick-witted planning. "Like I said, no one other than my family knows."

He paused, tried to control the tumbling in the pit of his stomach when he then said, "I'm engaged to be married."

The man looked shocked as he simply stared at Eli. Then Farmer narrowed his eyes in disbelief, sputtered and said, "Engaged? You? Impossible!"

Eli smiled. "Yes, sir. Me. Engaged. Why is that so hard to believe?"

"You're a Steele and from what I hear, you're the worst one in the pack when it comes to commitment."

Eli chuckled, refusing to acknowledge what Farmer had said was probably true. "People said the same thing about Galen. And as you recall it was hard for everyone to believe he got married, but you saw it with your own eyes since you attended the wedding."

Farmer nodded.

Thinking he was on a roll and might as well be convincing as possible, Eli leaned back in his chair and added, "All it takes is the right woman to come along to change a man's mind."

A huge smile then touched the man's features. "You're right about that. Me and my Claudia have been married for almost fifty years. And she's still the apple of my eye."

The man then relaxed back in his chair, definitely

a little more jovial. "Your announcement changes everything, Eli. I'm glad you've come to your senses and given up the endless parade of women. With a focused mind you'd make a great president of the council."

Eli smiled. Had he known it would have been this easy, he would have told the little white lie long ago. "Does that mean you'll consider supporting me in my bid for president?"

"Yes, once I see your engagement is legit and that you're not pulling my leg. Has a date been set? And just who is this woman you're marrying?"

Eli swallowed. He hadn't expected Farmer not to believe him or go further and question him about a name. "No, a date hasn't been set and I doubt that you know her."

The man waved off his words. "That very well might be the case but I expect to meet her sometime. My Claudia will probably want to have her over for tea or something and introduce her to the other wives. I don't know why the two of you are keeping your engagement a secret, however, to get my support you'd have to come out in the open about it. I want to meet her and I think the council's Thanksgiving party will be the perfect time and place to introduce her to everyone. And I don't like rushing things but since the elections are in January, I think a Christmas wedding would be nice. You can start off the year right with a wife."

Eli felt a tightening in his throat. He hadn't counted on the man suggesting something like that. "A Christmas wedding?"

"Yes. It's a wonderful time to marry. So tell me,

what's her name? Who is the woman who has captured the heart of the elusive Eli Steele?"

It was on the tip of his tongue to say such a woman didn't exist, but Eli knew saying such a thing would catch him as a bald-face liar. So he said the name of the only woman who'd been in his thoughts lately. Not only was she in them but she was dominating them.

"Stacey. Stacey Carlson."

And after saying the name, Eli knew he was now in one hot mess.

Stacey stood at her stove stirring the pot of stew she'd made. She'd cooked more than enough and would drop a container over at Cohen's tomorrow. The movers would be arriving soon to begin packing him up. He had made plans to move in with Tyson a few days after the party since her place was so small and Tyson lived close to the hospital.

And since Tyson had such a huge condo with a breathtaking view of the mountains, he had suggested that she have Cohen's going away party at his place. She had everything ordered for the party and now all the invitees had to do was show up on Saturday night, and there was no doubt in her mind that they would. Even Dee would be flying in Saturday morning to help her with any last-minute planning.

She couldn't help but smile when she thought about the number of customers who'd complimented her shop's holiday decorations. And sales had been extremely good today. In fact, she'd had to order more of the dancing Santa, which seemed to be a favorite, as well as the dancing Rudolph who wagged his short tail and blinked his red nose.

Turning the knob for the stew to continue to simmer, she grabbed the book she had begun reading off the table. It was an adventure thriller written by Rock Mason, one of her favorite authors, and just the type of book she needed to get her mind off Eli.

He hadn't dropped back in her shop that day and when she'd left for home she had noted his car was still in the parking lot. She shrugged, figuring he'd show back up when the time suited him, and the thought of him doing so didn't bother her in the least. She didn't have to remind herself that she and Eli were not in a committed relationship. She knew what side the bread was buttered on and didn't want things any other way. In fact, she looked forward to seeing him again in the morning. After the hot quickie they'd shared in her office, there was no doubt in her mind that he would be back.

An hour or so later she was stretched on the sofa reading her book when she heard the doorbell. A glance out the window indicated night had descended while she'd been engulfed in her novel. She shifted her gaze to the door when the doorbell sounded again and a rush of excitement moved up her spine.

She knew who had come visiting. She placed her book on the table, eased off the sofa and crossed the room to the door. A quick look out the peephole confirmed the sensations flowing through her body. It was Eli. Her heart began hammering in her chest and fire seemed to flare through her blood. What was there about him that could make her react this way? Make her a passionate being, one she didn't know existed but wanted to explore?

Suddenly feeling naughty, she ran her hand through the curls on her head, tossed her head back as a rueful grin touched her lips. Eli was here for one reason only, and she didn't have a problem with that reason. In fact, since she'd dropped the element of love from the mix of things for her, she felt better. She no longer had to worry about the possibility of her heart getting broken. There would be no more pain for her, and no sense of betrayal. She was determined to never have to worry about deception from another single male. From now on she would savor life, but not get bogged down in it.

Heaving a sensual sigh, she turned the knob to open the door.

When Stacey opened the door, Eli could only stand there a second and get his bearings. There was something about seeing her that was having some sort of effect on him. Yes, it was an arousing effect, but there was something else as well. Something he couldn't put a name to. Something that seemed to be going over his head—the one attached to his neck—and landing straight into another.

He shifted his stance and studied the smile on her lips. It was a warm smile. Inviting. Seductive. Instead of thinking he'd probably caught her at a bad time, for some reason he had a feeling he'd caught her at a good one.

He held her gaze. Felt the heat. Inhaled her scent. And the depth of his desire and need for her was sending blood rushing into every part of his body.

"Would you like to come in, Eli?"

He blinked, realizing he hadn't even said anything. Not even a greeting. The last time they'd seen each other had been that morning when he had made love to her in her office. "Yes, I'd like to come in."

She moved aside and he walked past her, fighting the urge to pull her into his arms, taste her lips and devour her mouth. He turned when he heard her close the door behind him. She was leaning against it wearing one of those short things again. A caftan was what they called it but it looked like pure seduction on her since it showed off her legs. Legs he loved to look at. Legs he loved having wrapped around him while they made love.

"Umm, I guess you just happened to be in the neighborhood, right?" she asked.

He eased his hands into the pockets of his jeans. That used to be the line he would give the women when he would show up unexpectedly for one of his famous booty calls. Did she assume that was what this was? When you think of it, she had no reason not to. And why did it suddenly bother him that she was so receptive to it, like the thought that he only wanted her for sex didn't irk her one iota.

"No, I didn't just happen to be in the neighborhood. When I left home I knew this was my destination," he said, being honest and wanting a reason to set the record straight.

She shrugged her shoulders. "The main thing is that you're here."

His gaze had shifted from her eyes to her lips and had watched them move. Her lips in action sent a sensuous shiver through his body and he felt himself get hard when he thought about several things he liked about her lips.

"Can I get you something?"

It wasn't what she asked but rather how she'd asked it that sent his heart pounding and his erection throbbing. He knew she had to see it since it was quite obvious he was hard for her. There was no way he could hide it now. "I'll take a beer if you have it. A cold one," he heard himself say. He needed a cold liquid to quell the heat flowing through his body.

"Sure, one beer coming up."

She walked by him. Deliberately brushed against him. Intentionally ignited his already hot and aroused body. Instantly it burst into flames. Without thinking, purely acting on instinct and need, he reached out for her and the moment her body was plastered to his, testosterone he couldn't control took over. Drove him over the edge.

On a masculine growl he pushed her down on the sofa and came down on top of her as a yearning and hunger so intense it had his teeth rattling, took over. He captured her mouth in his while his hands stripped her of her clothes in a need to touch her body, every single inch of her skin. And he wanted to taste it as well. She had the flavor of peaches and crème, he decided as his lips moved over her, savoring her with a hunger he felt in every muscle of his body.

When she was a hot, writhing mass of fire beneath him, he stood just long enough to strip off his own clothes and returned to her, easing between her legs and then entering her while her flames spread to engulf him. The moment he felt those familiar inner muscles clamp down on him, he exploded and screamed an orgasm. It was a full body climax and they were consumed by it. It was simply amazing. Hearing her scream his name made his heart clamor with pride.

Moments later, he tried breathing again as he eased off her and slumped down off the sofa to the floor and stared up at the ceiling. If this kept up, Stacey was going to be the death of him. Making such a claim about a woman was simply unheard of for Eli.

"Was it worth you stopping by, Eli?"

He snapped his head up to where she lay on the sofa naked, and in a position that invited a repeat performance of what they'd just done. He fought the urge. "This is not why I'm here, Stacey. I didn't come for this."

He'd said the words with more force than he'd intended and he watched her brow furrow, obviously confused by what he'd said. Easing to the edge of the sofa she propped herself up on her elbow to stare down at him.

"If you didn't come for this, then what did you come for, Eli?" she questioned in a surprised voice.

It was a voice that apprised him of what she assumed his expectations were of her, her role in his life, which was basically the same function as with any other woman he associated with. She was about to find out just how wrong that assumption was.

He pulled up his body while holding her gaze. When he got to within a breath of her lips, he spoke in a clear, distinct and serious voice.

"I came here tonight to ask you to marry me."

Chapter 14

Stacey was convinced if Eli hadn't been so close to break her fall that she would have tumbled right off the sofa. Instead, every breath was sucked from her lungs and every ounce of blood in her body suddenly rushed to her head.

Her reaction to what he'd said evidently was amusing, which would account for the smile that touched the corners of his lips. Now, she was equally convinced he had gone over the deep end.

"Marry you?" she somehow found her voice to ask.

"Yes, on Christmas Day."

Stacey frowned. "What have you been drinking, Eli? You don't love me and I don't love you. Why on earth would you suggest we marry? And besides that, you are *not* the marrying kind and we both know it." Deep in her heart, Stacey wished Eli did have intense feelings for her. It would have been wonderful if Eli sincerely wanted her as his future wife, but that was just a far-fetched fantasy.

She watched him eyeing her as he leaned back on his haunches. That too-serious look reclaimed his features. "Yes, we both know it." He didn't say anything for a minute and then asked, "Do you recall me mentioning that a friend of mine suggested that I consider doing the wife for hire thing to win the presidency of the business council?"

She nodded. "Yes, I remember."

"I decided to take his advice and do it."

His words had her looking at him like he was stone mad, but there was no help for it. He wasn't thinking rationally. People didn't pretend they were married to win elections.

She eased off the sofa and stood. Being naked and having this sort of conversation with him didn't jibe with her, so she dressed herself in the clothes he'd taken off. She knew he was watching her every move.

"I know what you're thinking," he said.

She glanced over at him while slipping on her caftan. "Do you?"

"Yes. You think what I'm doing is manipulating the process."

"And you don't?"

"No. I see it as a way to get what I want."

And Eli Steele always got what he wanted, she thought.

"Okay, you've decided to take your friend up on his idea and hire someone to be your wife to win the presidency of this business council. What does that have to do with me?"

He pulled himself to his feet to put on his own clothes. "Your name was the first to come to mind."

"As a possible wife?"

"Yes."

Stacey frowned as she went back to sit on the sofa, trying not to notice how sexy he looked slipping back into his briefs. "Let me explain something to you, Eli. What happened between me and my ex-fiancé left more than a bitter taste in my mouth regarding marriage. The old me used to walk around and see things through rose-colored glasses. Well, those glasses are now broken and I see things more clearly now. What I see is that marriage—pretend or otherwise—isn't for me."

"You haven't heard the deal I'm offering. I suggest you do so before turning down my proposal."

Stacey sighed and looked away, knowing what he was offering really didn't matter. She wasn't getting married for all the wrong reasons. She pushed to the back of her mind the thought that she'd once planned to get married for all the *right* reasons, yet she'd gotten screwed over anyway.

She leaned back against the sofa and crossed her legs. "Okay, Eli, what are you offering?"

He zipped up his pants and to Stacey, the sound seemed to echo all through the room. "For starters," he said, holding her gaze. "I will pay you one hundred thousand dollars."

Stacey's eyes widened. "One hundred thousand dollars?"

"Yes. And you'll retain ownership of anything—gifts or otherwise—that you get from me while we're engaged or married. I consider myself a very generous man."

Stacey nervously licked her lips. That she could believe. She doubted he had a selfish bone in his body, just several arrogant ones. She shook her head. "All that sounds good but I'm still not interested."

He inhaled what sounded like a frustrated breath as he belted his jeans. "Then what will it take for you to be interested? There has to be something you want that will convince you to change your mind."

There really wasn't, Stacey thought. There was nothing to make her want to share anything with a man other than what she was already doing with Eli. Now that she was getting the hang of this casual affair thing, she thought it wasn't so bad. No emotional entanglement was the only way to go. Her heart wasn't on the line and she didn't have to worry whether he was being faithful to her.

And now he was proposing marriage of all things. Not a real marriage, just a fake one if it got that far. But there would be an engagement and she knew far too well how those worked. At least she thought she did. Wallace had come with his own set of rules.

Out of curiosity, she asked, "What happens if I agree to do it?"

He slid into the wing chair opposite her. "We announce to family and friends we've decided to marry, which of course will garner a lot of surprise and questions. But I'll have a script prepared in advance so we'll know what to say."

Stacey nodded. She knew for sure that he would.

"And then," he continued, "nothing between us

changes other than we will be operating in the open pretending to be an engaged couple very much in love. In other words, we will have an exclusive relationship like we have now."

A look of surprise showed in her expression. "We've been having an exclusive relationship?"

He seemed surprised she would ask. "Yes. You thought I've been seeing other women while sleeping with you?"

She shrugged. "I really wasn't sure what you were doing, Eli. I didn't concern myself with such things. You assured me you were healthy and would stay that way. That was good enough for me." She could have sworn she'd seen something flash in the depths of his green eyes at her statement. But it was so quick she couldn't be certain.

"And then we will have a very private wedding on Christmas to make it seem that we want to ring in the New Year right," he added. "The election is the last week in January and you'll remain married to me for a full year after that. And just in case you're worried, the contractual terms of our marriage and subsequent divorce will not be drawn up by me to avoid any type of conflict of interest. I plan on using Jared Westmoreland. I'm sure you've heard of him."

Yes, she'd heard of the nationally known attorney who handled the divorce cases of a number of the rich and famous. "Yes, I've heard of him."

"Well, Jared happens to be the brother of my cousin-in-law. Quade Westmoreland is married to my cousin, Cheyenne, and they live in Charlotte. I called Jared to discuss my proposal before coming over here."

She looked at him skeptically. "And he didn't see anything strange about what you want to do?"

"No." Eli paused for a second and then said, "So now that you see my offer is on the up-and-up, I'll go back to what I asked earlier. Is there anything I can throw into the pot that will seal the deal?"

After a few quiet moments, Stacey glanced over at him. He was waiting on her answer. She decided to ask for something so ridiculous, something he wouldn't give up in a million years, just to stump him, make him think twice about ever proposing to her again. When an idea came into her head, she forced back the smile that threatened to spread across her lips.

"Yes, Eli, come to think of it, there is this one thing."

"What is it?"

"My shop. I really like it and think it's in a good location on the ground floor of your office building. It's a prime spot that draws in a lot of traffic and I know that's one of the main reasons I'm doing so well in sales. However, I'm paying you close to six thousand dollars each month for rental."

He nodded. "You want me to reduce the amount you pay to lease the space?"

A smile touched the corners of her lips. "No, I want to *own* the space."

He looked taken back. "Own it?"

"Yes, own it free and clear. It's just a few square feet out of many so you won't miss it. You'll still own the rest of the entire building." A satisfied look appeared on her face. He might want to be council president but he wouldn't want to get elected *that* bad. Everything had its limits and she'd heard he prided himself on owning such a prime piece of real estate in downtown Phoenix. He wouldn't readily share it with anyone.

He stared at her for what seemed like the longest time and she could imagine the wheels turning in his head. Let them turn. It shouldn't take long for him to realize he would do better making his offer of marriage to someone else.

"Fine."

She looked over at him. He had spoken in a somewhat quiet voice. "Fine, what?"

"I'll give you the shop. Free and clear. I'll have Jared include it in the agreement."

She was speechless. Her head began spinning. "You want the presidency of the business council that much?"

"Yes, it's an investment in my future. Besides, I'll also be getting you in the deal and you better believe I plan to make having you worth my while."

Eli leaned back in the chair and watched Stacey wear down her carpet by pacing back and forth. She still hadn't given him a final answer although he had conceded to her one concession. Doing so had left a bitter taste in his mouth but he figured it would all work out in the end. Sooner or later she would decide to join Cohen in Florida and when she did, he would make her a good offer for the space. He would just make sure Jared's contract gave him the first option to buy.

And speaking of Jared…

She had asked earlier if Jared had thought his proposal strange. What he didn't tell her was that Jared had found it rather amusing since he and his wife, Dana, had started out sharing a fake engagement and it had worked out fine. In the end, they'd fallen in love and had gotten married.

Eli knew for him and Stacey such a thing wouldn't be happening. She'd pegged him right earlier tonight when she'd said he wasn't the marrying kind. But he could certainly pretend to be. And he had no qualms pretending with her.

His gaze stayed on her legs as she walked back and forth. They were such a gorgeous pair. He took note of that each and every time he saw them uncovered. His eyes reluctantly strayed from her legs up to her face. He could tell she was still thinking and he couldn't help wondering what she was thinking about. Her answer should really be a no-brainer. He wasn't a bad catch and being engaged to him—pretend or otherwise—couldn't be all bad. But since she was still in her "weighing the options" mode, he decided to tip the scales in his favor.

"As your fiancé, I'll look forward to attending that party with you in Memphis."

She stopped walking and glanced over at him. Their gazes connected and he felt a hot rush consume his body. He didn't have to ponder what that was all about. Stacey could turn him on like nobody's business. "You would be willing to go with me?"

He smiled. "Of course. I'll officially be your fiancé so it wouldn't be as if you were lying to anyone. Besides, I want to see the jerk stupid enough to let you go."

She smiled but he hadn't made the comments to garner brownie points. He was dead serious. He needed to see this Wallace guy. The man certainly had more than a few screws loose.

She dropped back down on the sofa and crossed her legs again and he was definitely taking it all in. Remembering what was between those legs and how much enjoyment he got sampling it. His gaze then traveled up the rest of her body. But then he liked her breasts as well. The nipples fit perfectly in his mouth. He definitely like licking and sucking on them.

"Neither Cohen nor your brothers are going to believe it," she interrupted his thoughts by saying. "As far as they know, we aren't even involved that way and now you're proposing that we marry around the holidays?"

He grinned slyly. "Yes. It will be our job to convince them we're madly in love. Just think of how much more relieved Cohen will be to leave you behind knowing you're engaged to me."

A skeptical look showed on her face. "He also knows your reputation as a ladies man."

"Yes, but my job is to convince your brother, as well as those on the business council, that I'm a changed man. I no longer embody the playboy image. Now I take on the role of a man who has fallen in love and intends to marry and settle down."

He glanced at his watch. It was getting late. "I much prefer an answer tonight, but if you feel you need to sleep on it then go right ahead. I'd like your decision by tomorrow. If you decide to go along with my plan then we can surprise everyone and make the announcement at your brother's going away party this weekend. That will make Cohen feel a little more comfortable leaving for Florida without you. He will know you'll be not only left in my care, but the care of all the other Steeles since we're a close family and Cohen knows it."

What he didn't say was that it would also effectively remove her from Tyson's care and protection.

"I will have to sleep on it, Eli. There's a lot I need to think about."

"Okay."

"And I promise to give you a decision as soon as I make one."

"That's fine." He eased up from his seat. "But just so you'll know, Harry Farmer caught me off guard when he came to visit me today and when I felt pressured into telling him I was an engaged man, he asked for a name. I gave him yours."

She narrowed her eyes at him. "You gave him my name and told him we were engaged to be married?"

"Yes. I was backed up against the wall and you were the first woman I thought about, mainly because you'd been on my mind all day. Hell, you've been on my mind every day…for quite some time."

He hadn't meant to tell her all that but it was the truth, although he wasn't all that happy about it. No woman had ever dominated his thoughts that much and the very idea that he couldn't control it from happening did not sit well with him. The thought of marrying her wouldn't be so bad as long as they understood each other and he was certain that they did.

When he'd read his horoscope this morning, it had said that by the end of the day he would have what his heart desired most. And now that the presidency was so close to his reach, he knew his horoscope prediction was true.

Chapter 15

Eli Steele wanted to marry her.

Stacey scowled as she stared at her reflection in the mirror while applying night cream to her face. He had to be desperate to even consider doing such a thing, which meant he wanted to be president of that council pretty bad.

She took a measured breath and decided although she'd told him she needed to think about it, there was nothing to think about. She wouldn't do it. He needed to find some other woman to do the honors.

First of all, nobody would believe that he of all people was ready to settle down with a wife, so he needed to come up with another plan to win over those people on the business council before election time. Over the years, he had painted a pretty good picture of who he was and what he was and people knew a leopard didn't change his spots overnight.

Besides, she thought, as she walked through the house to lock up for the night, she was the last woman he should want to marry. But then as she set her alarm, she remembered that he had no intentions of staying married. One year. Just long enough for him to clinch the presidency and then get comfortable in the position.

But he had brought up a good point. If they could convince Cohen their engagement was legit, then her brother would leave for Florida believing that he'd left her in good hands, even if they were the hands of a former playboy. And Eli had definitely sweetened the pot by agreeing to throw in ownership of her shop. Although she could tell that her suggestion had been a bitter pill for him to swallow, he'd done so anyway.

A short while later she was about to slide into bed when her phone rang. She smiled when she saw the caller was Dee. "Hey, girl."

"What's going on, Stace?"

"Nothing much. What's going on with you?"

Dee gave her an update on little Tommy's torment of Melissa as well as the other kids in her kindergarten class. Although Dee complained about her students getting on her last nerve at times, Stacey knew Dee enjoyed what she did for a living.

Just like she enjoyed doing what she did for a living. Being stuck in a nine-to-five job hadn't been what she'd wanted, but it had paid the bills. But now she liked getting up every morning and going into her shop because, other than the lease payment every month, it was hers. And now Eli was giving her a chance to get rid of even the lease payments. She would own the shop free and clear if she was to marry him.

Was it worth it?

She tried to think of how it would be married to Eli. There was no doubt she would be the envy of a lot of women since he was considered a prime catch. And there was no doubt in her mind what their sleeping arrangements would be—basically the same as they were now—whenever, wherever and however they liked.

So why was she having misgivings about his offer when it was nothing more than a business proposal? Especially when it could be a win-win situation for her. She was sexually attracted to him. Evidently, they were sexually attracted to each other. They had both acknowledged they didn't love each other, so there was no risk of her heart getting broken. So what was causing her to flatly refuse his offer? Maybe it was because she was starting to feel a deeper attraction toward him, but it was something she didn't want to admit.

"Okay, Stace, what's going on with you?"

Stacey blinked when she heard what Dee had asked. "What makes you think something is going on with me?"

"Because you zoned out on me several times like your thoughts were a million miles away and not on what I was saying. It's not like you not to be focused."

Stacey would have to agree that she hadn't been listening to what Dee had been saying. As usual, her thoughts were on Eli.

"Stace?"

She began nibbling on her bottom lip thinking she needed a second opinion, and since Dee had a level head most of the time, she would confide in her best friend. Stacey cleared her throat. “I’ve been involved in an affair,” she came right out and said.

There was a pause and then Dee said, “Does that mean you’ve finally gotten over Wallace?”

Stacey inwardly sighed. Dee and Cohen would be surprised to learn getting over Wallace hadn’t been that hard, which made her wonder just how much she was really into Wallace anyway. “Yes, and to be quite honest with you, it was more my pride than my heart that was broken.”

“I know. A woman’s pride means everything and the last thing she’d want is for a man to trample it, especially a man you trusted. So who is the man who convinced you to live again? And is it serious?”

Stacey chuckled. “No, it’s not serious, just a case of intense lust. No emotional entanglements.”

“Is that how you want it, Stace? You used to believe in—”

“Something I found out was just a fairy tale. There’s no such thing as true love or forever-after, Dee. I realize that now.”

“I disagree since I’m still holding out on that possibility, but we won’t argue that point tonight. So who is he?”

Stacey drew in a deep breath. “Eli Steele.”

After leaving Stacey’s place, Eli felt like he needed a stiff drink and intended to drop by Morgantown and have one. But then he decided he wanted company while he tried clearing his head, so he found himself going across town to where Galen lived.

As usual, Brittany was glad to see him, although

Galen pretended to be annoyed by his visit. While Galen poured him a glass of bourbon, his drink of choice, he listened while Brittany told him how her school of etiquette, the one she'd opened here in Phoenix, was doing. Already all her classes were full and she had hired three new teachers.

And while they talked, Eli couldn't help noticing how his brother and sister-in-law interacted. It wasn't the first time he'd noticed, but it was the first time his mind and thoughts had zeroed in on it. It was still hard to believe that his once die-hard bachelor brother had transformed into a husband who cherished the very ground his wife walked on. It was obvious in the way Galen looked at Brittany and it was clear as glass he didn't give a damn who noticed. They made a perfect couple and Eli couldn't recall ever seeing his brother happier. He then thought about the conversation he and Galen had shared in his office a few days ago and pushed the memory to the back of his mind.

"So are you going to sit there and drink all my bourbon or are you going to tell me what's on your mind, Eli?"

Eli glanced around and noticed Brittany had left. He then recalled she'd told him good-night a half hour ago. "There's nothing on my mind."

Galen laughed. "Who are you kidding? You never just drop by. Whenever you come to visit, it's with the others, rarely alone, so what's going on, Eli?"

Galen's frown served as a warning when he added, "And don't give me some smart-ass response. I'm not in the mood."

Eli had thought about doing that very thing and

kicked the idea out of his mind real quick. Galen was the oldest and the other five respected him as such, which was why Eli was here. He and Galen might butt heads every once in a while, but if Eli needed to discuss anything and get a serious answer, it was Galen whom he sought out. For one thing, Galen knew how to keep his mouth shut about anything he would tell him.

He gave Galen a serious look. "I asked a woman to marry me."

If he had expected his brother to drop the wineglass from his hand or roll over in shock, then he was sorely disappointed. In fact, none of Galen's features registered surprise and for some reason that annoyed Eli. "I didn't get the response from you that I expected, Galen," he said, taking a sip of his drink.

"What kind of response did you expect when you've already told me about the woman? Although you didn't give me her name, you told me enough for me to know you'd fallen in love with her."

Eli nearly choked on his drink. When his throat had sufficiently gotten cleared and his coughing had ceased, he glanced over at eyes identical to his and glared. "What the hell are you talking about? I'm not in love!"

Galen leaned forward in his chair and pinned him with a direct stare. "I assumed you were since you asked the woman to marry you. And I also assumed she's the same woman you're so attracted to that you can't think straight. The same one you dream about at night and then have naughty fantasies of in the mornings. The same woman that you think you couldn't function until you've had a piece of. The same woman who can make you feel better than anything you thought possible in the bedroom. And the same woman you can't wait to see again. To be with again."

Eli opened his mouth to say something, and then he shut it tight. Damn Galen for having a great memory and recalling every single thing he'd told him. He sat there silent for a moment, literally pissed that Galen had used Eli's own words against him. Just because Galen might have endured similar lustful thoughts for Brittany before falling in love with her meant nothing. He and his brother were two different men. Brittany and Stacey were two different women.

But both had caught the eye of a Steele man.

Eli's hand trembled somewhat as he took another sip of his drink. That wasn't strong enough so he then took a huge gulp and felt the bourbon burn his throat going down. But he needed it.

"You drink any more of that and it will be the guest room for you tonight, Eli," Galen warned in a serious tone. "What you should do is stop trying to fight the inevitable. You've fallen in love. Admit it. And I still want to know if you don't think you've fallen in love, then why would you ask the woman to marry you?"

Eli sat his glass on the table between them with a thump. "I have not fallen in love, Galen, so stop saying that. And the reason I asked her to marry me is strictly business. I need to clean up my image to win the council presidency, so we're going to pretend that we are engaged."

Galen's brow lifted. "A pretended engagement?"

"Yes. And we'll marry on Christmas Day and stay married for a year. Not a day longer."

Galen shook his head. "I assume this was your idea."

Eli smiled. "No, it really was Lex's and when he first suggested it, I thought he'd lost his mind. But now I agree doing such a thing has merit." There was no need to tell Galen that Harry Farmer's visit had prompted him to think that way.

"And your woman has agreed?"

Eli's lips spread into a thoughtful smile at the idea of Stacey being his woman. He hadn't thought of her as such before now, but he liked the title. He thought it fit. "Not yet, but she's thinking about it."

Galen nodded. "Who is she? Who is the woman who has you acting besotted even if you claim you aren't?"

Eli shifted in his chair. Galen wasn't going to like what he was about to say, but he didn't care. It was what it was, and Stacey was an adult. "The woman is Stacey. Stacey Carlson."

"Eli Steele?" Dee sputtered as if she'd been drinking.

"Yes."

"Hold up, Stace. Time out. Are you saying you're involved with one of those Steeles? One of those guys who you know don't have a serious bone in their bodies? Who don't know the meaning of commitment? One of those 'Bad News' Steeles?"

"Yes. That's what I'm saying."

"But why, when you know he doesn't mean you any good?"

"Because like I said, I'm no longer looking at life through rose-colored glasses. So far, Eli has given me just what I want."

"Which is?"

"Fun without any expectations. No emotional entanglements. And now he wants to sweeten the pot."

"In what way?" Dee asked in a voice that said she was almost afraid to.

"He wants to give me a Steele for Christmas."

"A what?" Dee asked confused.

She then took the next ten minutes to go into details about Eli's outlandish offer. It would not have taken that long if Dee hadn't interrupted her every few minutes asking questions. And she still had more.

"So the two of you will only be married a year?" Dee asked as if weighing her answers.

"Yes."

"And he'll pay you one hundred thousand dollars, throw in ownership of your shop—free and clear—as well as let you keep any gifts you acquire during the lifetime of the marriage?"

"Yes."

"And you didn't say…I'm asking since I'm dying of curiosity. Is he any good in bed?"

Dee's question triggered memories that ignited Stacey's brain. Hot, potent, mind-blowing memories, especially of the one that morning in her office as well as the time here tonight. She was convinced he had heated passion flowing through every vein in his body. The man's fingers and tongue should be outlawed and his male anatomy should be considered a highly dangerous weapon.

"Yes, he's good," she answered honestly. "In fact, if he was any better I'd probably be dead."

Dee giggled. "Well, you certainly answered my

question, so when do you want me to fly in for the wedding?"

Stacey blinked. "There will not be a wedding."

"Why not? A Steele for Christmas sounds pretty darn good to me. And you have to admit he's offering a pretty good package deal. Good-looking man. Great sex. Nice piece of change. You get to own your shop. And you get a wedding ring on your finger for a year. You know what my granny used to say. 'A woman should change her name even if it's for one day.' A divorcée sounds a heck of a lot better than a spinster in my book."

Stacey nibbled on her bottom lip. She hadn't considered things that way.

"And you can bring him to my parents' anniversary party and be telling the truth when you say that he's your fiancé. I can just imagine the look on Gail's face when she realizes that she got the frog and you got the prince."

Stacey burst out laughing. Dee certainly had a way with words.

"Do you know what I would do if I were you?" Dee asked her.

Stacey was almost afraid to ask. "No, what would you do?"

"I would give Eli Steele the best year of his life and make doubly sure that while doing so I'm getting the best year of mine."

"Your pacing is giving me a crook in my neck, Galen," Eli said, staring across the room at his brother.

Eli rubbed that same neck while wondering why he

was still there. He should have left to go home long ago. He had to go to work in the morning while Galen didn't. His brother worked from home, right in his garage, creating those million-dollar video games. Usually this was his most relaxing time of the year, when all the games Galen had worked hard on all year hit the stores in time for the holidays.

"Better a sore neck than a kicked ass," Galen said, glaring. "Because that's what Cohen will do when he finds out that you've been involved with Stacey."

"She's a grown woman."

"And you're a Steele. Cohen knows us well. He knows how the five remaining Steele brothers operate." Galen then rubbed his chin thoughtfully. "But you have asked Stacey to marry you and that's a good thing. It will definitely show commitment on your part…even if the whole marriage is a sham."

"True. The only people who won't know it's the real thing is me, you, Stacey and Brittany. I only threw Britt in because I figure you probably tell your wife everything."

Galen smiled, unashamedly. "True."

Eli rolled his eyes. "Oh, yeah, and Jared also knows."

Galen lifted a brow. "Jared knows?"

"Yes. He's handling the divorce on the back end."

Galen simply stared at him.

"What?" Eli asked.

"Nothing."

Eli scowled. "Apparently there is something, Galen, or you wouldn't be looking at me that way."

"I can't believe you're doing this," Galen said.

"I'm going to do it if Stacey agrees. It will clinch

the presidency for me and get Mom off my back for a while. You can't do better than that."

"Yes, you can. You can make it a real marriage."

Eli looked aghast. "Why would I want to do a thing like that?"

What Eli thought was a silly-looking grin touched Galen's lips. "I bet by the time the wedding comes around you'll have figured it out."

Chapter 16

The next morning, when Stacey got to work, she saw Eli's car already parked in the reserved space. Evidently, he'd needed to get some work done and had come to the office early, she surmised, cutting off her car's ignition and getting out of her car.

She glanced at her watch. It wasn't even quite eight o'clock yet. She hadn't been able to sleep last night and figured she would get to the shop early and put out the huge Styrofoam candy canes that had arrived late yesterday.

Everyone who'd entered her shop had commented on how festive it was, perfect for the holidays. Only Mr. Jones, who owned the optometrist shop on the second floor, had complained saying he felt she'd put up the Christmas decorations too early since nobody had celebrated Thanksgiving yet.

Her thoughts then shifted back to Eli since they were

rarely off him anyway. And he had pretty much admitted the same thing about her. She figured that lust was a powerful thing. It had the ability to make rational people act irrationally.

And last night and this morning she was still thinking irrationally and blamed Dee for it. Her best friend had set her mind in motion and definitely given her a lot of food for thought. And once she'd slept on it, or at least tried to, she had to agree that marrying Eli for just a year wouldn't be such a bad idea. And considering she would get to own her shop in the end, it was really a smart thing to do.

Eli would not be a hard man for any woman to easily fall in love with but she didn't have to worry about doing something as foolish as that. She was grateful that although she was a weakling when it came to his body, she would never allow herself to succumb to his seductive powers or persuasive charms. Marriage to him wouldn't change a thing. She couldn't get any more attracted to him than she was now and since she would never trust any man with her heart ever again, she knew her limitations .

Stacey's steps slowed when she entered the building and saw Eli. He was leaning against the door of her shop and it was obvious he was waiting on her. She gave him a thoughtful look as heat suffused her body. She knew why he was there. The look in his eyes said it all.

No matter what her answer would be to his outlandish wedding proposal, they would share this nonetheless. They were too intimately into each other, too physically attracted not to. And heaven help her, anticipation was rushing through her bloodstream.

"Good morning, Eli," she said softly, upon reaching her door.

"Good morning, Stacey."

She wished the texture of his voice didn't feel like warm honey all over her skin. "You're early."

"Yes," he said, his green eyes holding hers as he reached out to take the key from her hand. "I was waiting for you."

Stacey swallowed. There was no reason to ask if there was something in particular that he wanted since the look in his eyes said it all. He planned to engage in some early morning delight. Was this how it would be to be married to him? Would she wake up to the promise of scorching-hot lovemaking?

"You look nice," he complimented her by saying, while his gaze swept over her. She felt it like an intimate caress.

"Thanks."

"You smell good, too."

"Thanks again."

He opened the door. "After you," he said.

She didn't say anything as she walked into her shop and turned off the alarm. She heard the sound of him locking the door and when she reached for the light switch, he said. "Don't bother."

He then captured her hand in his as he pulled her around the corner to an area of her shop hidden from view and behind a string of silver bells, overhanging Christmas holly and a cluster of holiday lights.

"Didn't we do this just last night? This is crazy," she muttered, but didn't snatch her hand from his.

"Crazy but needed," he muttered back. "I couldn't sleep for thinking of you and wanting this," he said.

Already he had her backed up against the wall, was pulling up her skirt, pulling down her panties and unzipping his pants. She decided to reach down and offer her assistance and do something else in the process.

Stacey gently shoved him down on the huge ornament storage box and leaned down over him. "You have slow fingers, Eli," she said, pushing his hand out the way and easing down his zipper. Her face was right there below his waist and the moment she lowered his zipper, the clean, masculine scent of him slid through her nostrils and heated her insides.

She licked her lips while studying the object of perfection that she held in her hand. It was awesome, magnificent, a nice work of art, darn pleasing to the eyes and temptation to her lips. Concentrating on the latter and not able to help herself, she lowered her mouth and took him inside.

Eli just knew he'd died mainly because this had to be how heaven felt. And the thought of his aroused member easing between her lips was just as mind-boggling as easing between her legs. But he would concentrate on this for now as she tortured him, clamping her mouth down on him and driving him crazy.

And when she began tonguing him, he reached out, grabbed a fistful of her hair to hold her mouth in place as she went to work on him. She was right. This was crazy. Madness at its worst but it was also pleasure at its best. And as her mouth moved all over him he knew she intended to drive him insane. She acted as if she was hungry for him. Literally starving. Sensations whipped through him and he thought he would come at any minute. His testicles tightened in anticipation. And in something else as well.

He gritted his teeth and threw his head back. "I'm trying not to come," he snarled through clenched teeth.

She gently fingered one of his testicles in a way that said *don't hold back, I want you to come. Now.*

So he did and forced the scream back down his throat. His pulse throbbed as every pore in his body seemed to open, become shrouded in sensuality. And she drew everything out of him.

"Oh, Stacey." And while the orgasm was still flowing in his veins, he shifted, pushed her back beneath him onto the box and eased between her legs. And when he had entered her, he whispered, "Lock your legs around me, baby."

And then he began riding her, pounding into her with reckless abandon. He rocked back and forth as his shaft throbbed to life inside of her. Every nerve in his body tingled and then something within him snapped. And for the first time in his life he felt a woman, actually felt her in a way he'd never felt one before. All the way in his blood.

And then his body jerked in another orgasm when she cried out his name in her own pleasure. And as he continued to pound hard into her satiny flesh, he knew something monumental had taken place just now. But he was in no frame of mind to try and figure out what.

* * *

"I've made my decision, Eli."

Barely able to catch his breath, Eli rolled off her. Sunlight coming in through a skylight overhead made him blink. At the same time, an uncomfortable stirring erupted low in his belly. He hadn't expected a decision from her so soon and that could only mean she was turning down his offer.

His gaze swept over to her face, studied it for a moment. Her eyes were closed and her features had the look of sensual bliss. His lips curled in a satisfied smile knowing he was responsible for that look. "And what is your decision?" he asked huskily, as his gaze shifted to her lips. He was tempted to lean over and taste them again. Hell, why was he so obsessed with her? Why couldn't he get enough?

She slowly opened her eyes and his met hers. "I will marry you," she said softly.

He battled for control as his heart did a happy dance. His body jolted in supreme delight. Something inside of him warned him not to question his blessings, but he couldn't help doing so. "Why did you decide to do it?"

She didn't say anything for a moment and then she explained, "I'd rather be a divorcée than grow older as an old maid."

He thought about what she'd said, just what she'd meant. "In other words, it's better to marry and divorce than not to have married at all?"

"Yes."

He glanced back up at the skylight. Strangely, it bothered him that though they hadn't married yet, she was already planning their divorce. Almost counting on it. Irritation swept through his bloodstream at the thought.

Eli checked his watch. "We need to get dressed," he said, getting to his feet and then helping her up. He reached down and handed her the panties he'd taken off her earlier.

"Thanks."

Great view, he thought as he watched her lift her skirt to slide them over her hips. Everything about her was luscious.

"So what's next? Do you still want to make our announcement at Cohen's going away party this weekend?" she asked.

"Not unless you want to tell Cohen beforehand and not catch him off guard."

Silence fell between them and he could tell she was considering his suggestion. A low stirring went through his gut at the way she was nibbling on her bottom lip and how her brows seem to arch together whenever her expression turned serious. His gaze then shifted back to her mouth and he felt blood rush through his veins at the illicit memory of what her mouth had done to him a short while ago.

He had a feeling her mouth would be imprinted on that particular body part for life. He then forced the very thought from his mind. No woman could make that kind of an impression on him. That wasn't possible.

"Either way, he's going to have a hard time believing it," she finally said, breaking into his thoughts.

Eli nodded. "Same goes for my family. But we'll just have to do our best and be convincing."

She stared at him, all wide-eyed. "And how will we do that?"

He couldn't help smiling as he reached out and gently brushed the back of his hand against her soft cheek. "Just follow my lead that night, sweetheart."

Chapter 17

Since she was the hostess, Stacey had arrived at the party site early with Dee in tow. Her best friend had flown in that morning and had shown up on her doorstep at the exact moment Eli was about to leave after having spent the night.

Stacey's cheeks warmed at the difference just a few days had made. Since deciding to execute their plan to announce their engagement and pending marriage, they had spent more time together than before.

He continued to show up at her shop each morning for a hot and titillating quickie, as well as drop by her place in the evening. She had gotten into the routine of expecting his visits and would have dinner prepared. It was during those times that she would get to see another side of Eli, when he would discuss his various cases with her while they shared a meal.

And she would tell him about her life back in Memphis and about her aunt Maggie and how she had helped raise her when her mother had died. If he'd gotten bored with the conversations, he'd never let on.

They had decided that they would live in his place after they married and when she mentioned she would continue to pay for the lease on her own apartment and keep it intact, since she would be returning there in a year's time, he had agreed with that arrangement.

Now she glanced across Tyson's living room and smiled when she saw Dee and Cohen standing alone talking. Dee had loved Cohen forever and she had a feeling that Cohen had feelings for Dee, although he'd never admitted such a thing.

Stacey figured he was allowing his belief that he was way too old for Dee get in the way. She thought a ten-year age difference wasn't a big deal. Besides, Dee always acted more mature than her years. Even Cohen had commented on that very thing numerous times.

She knew Dee was tired of Cohen not making a move and would make her own move soon, which was probably why she was over there offering to fly to Florida to help him settle in. Stacey could only wish her best friend the best of luck with her game plan.

She glanced at her watch and wondered why Eli hadn't arrived yet. All of his brothers, as well as his parents, were here already. His mother had approached her a few minutes ago to compliment her on how well she'd put the party together. She'd also heard from several people how beautiful the holiday display was in her shop, and she would have to drop by one day and see it.

Stacey took a sip of her wine as she studied Eli's parents. They were the epitome of a happy couple who had spent over thirty years together, and it was evident that they were still very much in love. And she could understand why. Eden Tyson Steele was a former internationally known model who looked half her age. The woman was simply beautiful and elegant. And Drew Steele was a very handsome man who'd passed those genes on to his six sons.

And as Stacey continued to observe the couple and how they interacted with each other, she knew there was more that held their marriage together than just great looks. There was also that chemistry that radiated between them that she could feel from across the room. The same heated chemistry she detected between Galen and his wife, Brittany.

She had met Brittany Thrasher Steele when Stacey had first moved to Phoenix and found her to be friendly and very likable. That was good since Brittany would be her sister-in-law for at least a year. She hated deceiving everyone into thinking she and Eli were marrying because they were madly in love but that had been part of the agreement they'd made.

Stacey nervously nibbled on her bottom lip. Not for the first time this week she wondered if she had done the right thing in consenting to marry him. Although he seemed pretty confident, she was convinced that no one was going to believe they were madly in love and had kept their relationship a secret until tonight...when they would announce their engagement.

Less than a half hour later while standing talking to Cohen, Dee and Mercury, she felt a stirring in the pit of her stomach. She glanced across the room and her gaze landed on Eli the moment he entered the house.

Her pulse began racing upon seeing him, dressed casually in a crisp blue shirt and pleated dark slacks.

He looked handsome. Good enough to eat. Savor. Enjoy. Her breath caught on all of the above and she couldn't help noticing the interest of several single female doctors, all colleagues of Cohen's, who'd been invited. At that moment, something happened that she hadn't expected. Her heart rate increased as a tinge of green jealousy flowed through her bloodstream. What on earth was wrong with her? She had no reason to be jealous of any woman where Eli was concerned. It wasn't as if they were in love or anything. Although she would admit that this week she had enjoyed her time with him so much that every once in a while she had to remind herself that nothing had changed and they were still emotionally detached.

"He looks hot," Dee leaned over and whispered for her ears only.

Stacey had to agree. Eli Steele *was* hot. And as she continued to stare over at him, he scanned the room, and when their gazes connected she felt her nipples harden against her blouse.

He had specifically asked her to wear a skirt and blouse tonight, without giving her a specific reason why, other than saying he got turned on looking at her legs. Considering how he would act sometimes whenever he saw them, she could believe him.

She swallowed thickly when he began moving toward her, pausing briefly to speak with his parents. Moments later when he continued toward her, she felt the sudden urge to run. But she stood still. She knew their playacting was about to begin.

* * *

Something, Eli wasn't sure what exactly, had his heart pounding in his chest. It had been doing so since the moment his gaze had lit on Stacey, picking her out in the crowded room.

She looked beautiful and had done just what he'd asked by wearing a skirt and blouse. It was a pretty pink blouse with lace trim at the hem and a short black pencil skirt. The outfit looked ultra-feminine on her and the skirt, which hit above the knee, showed off a pair of beautiful legs. The most gorgeous pair any woman could ever own. Her body—in or out of clothes—was what fantasies were made of.

But there was more to it than just his physical attraction to her, more to his obsession with her legs. They had spent a lot of time together this week and all of it hadn't been in the bedroom. And at that moment he knew what it was. He sucked in a deep breath and nearly lost his step when the truth hit him right between the eyes. Galen had been right. He *had* fallen in love with her.

Damn, damn and triple damn.

He had begun putting the bits and pieces of the puzzle together this week. There had to be a reason he would seek her out every single chance he got just for the feel of not only thrusting into her body, but for the ultimate, overwhelming sensation he felt whenever he would shoot off inside of her. Sharing the very essence of him with her.

He had spent enough time with Stacey to know how she felt about love and commitment. No emotional entanglements. He'd heard it from her several times and for a while he'd agreed with her. Therefore, he knew he had his work cut out for him, but then he hadn't wanted to fall in love with her. It just happened and he had no regrets. But the fall of Eli would cost her. He intended to make her a victim just like him. Willing or not.

"Good evening, everyone," he greeted, coming to a stop in front of the small group, but deliberately beside Stacey. Everyone returned his greeting.

"I was beginning to think you wouldn't be showing up," Mercury said, eyeing his brother curiously.

"There was no way I would have missed it," Eli said. His gaze then went to Stacey. "May I speak with you privately for a moment, Stacey?"

He saw the look of surprise and curiosity in both Cohen and Mercury's features. Then there was the look of downright amusement in Dee's. Cohen and Mercury were probably wondering what on earth he needed to talk to Stacey about. As far as either of them knew, they were merely acquaintances, definitely not what one would consider as friends.

"Sure, Eli," Stacey said, smiling up at him.

And Eli baffled both her brother and his even further when he took her hand as they moved toward the French doors leading to the patio.

Stacey's heart began racing the moment they were outside. In a darkened area of the patio, Eli pulled her into his arms and kissed her. She returned it so hungrily, giving in to the sensations swamping her. Sensations Eli could stir so easily.

She heard the groan that rattled in his throat, felt the hardness of his erection at the juncture of her legs as his hand cupped her backside while grinding his body against hers.

He was devouring her, reminding her of some of the benefits of marrying him, staying on as his wife for hire for a year. That meant twelve months of physical pleasure. Twelve months of letting herself go, indulging and becoming the sensuous woman she knew she could be. The sensuous woman she wanted to be.

He slowly pulled away from her mouth and on the dimly lit patio she could barely make out his features. But she didn't have to see him to know desire was flaring in the depths of his eyes. And although she didn't see him clearly, she did hear him when he whispered in a deep, husky tone, "I love you, Stacey."

She looked at him questioningly and then glanced around. Although she didn't see anyone outside on the patio with them, she figured there must have been someone within close range. Someone Eli wanted to hear his pretend words of love. In that case, she decided to go along with the program. "And I love you, too, Eli."

He surprised her even further when he linked her fingers into his and asked, "Will you marry me?"

She paused for a moment. He had already asked her to marry him. He was definitely laying it on thick to repeat the question, but if that's what he felt he had to do for appearances' sake then who was she to argue? "Yes, I'll marry you."

At that moment she felt him slide a ring onto her finger and she glanced down. She couldn't make out the design in the darkness but she saw the diamond sparkle in the moonlight. She blinked. The size of the diamond appeared large but she knew she had to be mistaken. It wasn't like they were sharing a real engagement so the ring he gave her wouldn't matter. There was no way he would spend a lot of money on a ring she was destined to keep. It was part of their arrangement that she didn't have to return any gift he gave her including the engagement ring.

"Now it's official," he said, reclaiming her attention. "And we'll marry on Christmas Day."

Again she wondered why he was repeating what they'd already decided on that week. But if he needed to be reassured that she hadn't changed her mind, then she would confirm what he'd said. "Yes, we'll marry on Christmas Day."

His fingers tightened around hers. "Come on, let's go tell the others."

She dismissed the excitement she heard in his voice and figured the sooner he could let people know they were engaged, the sooner people would assume he had cleaned up his playboy image, which was important to him. And that was the only reason he was marrying her in the first place.

When they walked back through the French doors, coming in from the darkened patio, she blinked at the bright lights and noticed several people had turned to glance their way. Apparently, they had seen him lead her out onto the patio and had wondered what was going on. Some of the women were staring at her and began whispering.

She was about to ask Eli what was going on when he spoke up loud enough for everyone to hear. "May I have your attention, please. Stacey and I have an announcement to make."

The room suddenly got quiet and everyone, those not doing so already, stopped what they were doing and turned to stare. When Eli was satisfied all eyes were on them, he then said, "I know this is going to come as a surprise to some of you, especially to you, Cohen. But Stacey and I have been seeing each other for a while now and it didn't take long for me to realize she's the woman I want in my life. I've asked her to marry me and she's accepted and we plan to marry on Christmas Day."

Pandemonium broke out. At least among some. Eli's brothers, as well as Cohen, just stood there with shocked looks on their faces. Eli's parents, initially just as shocked, quickly recovered and smiled, as if pleased with the announcement.

Dee was the first person to rush over and hug her. Stacey whispered to Dee, "What's going on? Why are those women staring at me like that?"

She noticed several of the women in the room were still openly staring like she'd grown two heads or something. Did they think her decision to marry Eli was a crazy one?

Dee threw her head back and laughed. "It's not you they're staring at per se, but it's that rock on your hand. It blinded everyone the moment you walked back inside off the patio. Your ring is simply gorgeous."

Stacey realized that she hadn't really taken a good look at her ring. She glanced down at her hand and her breath caught in her throat. She nearly passed out in shock. She couldn't believe what she was seeing.

The ring he had slid onto her finger was the same one that she'd seen that day in the jewelry store window within the Christmas display. A ring by Zion. And it suddenly dawned on her that the one ring she had wished for was now hers.

"When did the two of you start seeing each other?"

"Why did you keep it a secret?"

"Why the rush on the wedding?"

Questions began hitting Eli all at once. Well prepared, he answered them easily, without missing a beat, while keeping his gaze on Stacey. She was staring down at the ring he'd given her. Did she not like it? Did she think it was too large? Too gaudy?

He had seen it the other day in the store window and he'd known it was hers. There was something about it that had made him immediately think of her and he had wanted to be the one to put it on her finger. And he had.

He had deliberately asked her to marry him, just like he'd intentionally told her he loved her. He was well aware she didn't love him nor had a clue he'd told her the truth. He did love her. But he had to prove to her that he wanted to clean up his image more than just to become president of the business council. More than anything he wanted to clean up his image for her as well. Earning her love was more important than anything.

"Your father and I are happy for you and Stacey," his mother came up to say, smiling brightly. "I can't wait to get to know Stacey better. Already I admire the woman who was able to knock you off your high horse."

He didn't respond to his mother's comments or that "I told you so" look in her eyes. He was relieved when she and his dad gave Stacey huge hugs and then moved on. He then leaned over and whispered to Stacey, "As you can see our engagement announcement has made my mother's night."

"Would the two of you like to tell me why I've been clueless about this?"

His gaze shifted from Stacey and met Cohen's questioning look. He had known Cohen long enough to know although he was smiling, the smile didn't quite reach his eyes. And he figured Cohen wouldn't be satisfied until he knew for certain Stacey was in good hands. Sincere hands. Eli understood and had expected Cohen's doubt.

Tyson, Mercury, Jonas and Gannon were standing with Cohen and although they weren't saying anything, it was obvious they wanted answers as well. Stacey had heard her brother's question and slid to Eli's side to give a united front. He appreciated her for doing that.

A party was still going on and Eli knew no matter what concerns Cohen might have, he wouldn't cause a scene. Eli intended to give him no reason to want to do so. "My goal was to win Stacey's heart and the last thing I needed was interference from any of you who think you know me so well. Those who thought I wasn't ready to give up the single life and settle down."

His comment seemed to make Cohen relax somewhat but he could tell from his brothers' expressions they weren't buying it.

"So Eli is the reason you didn't want to follow me to Florida," Cohen said to Stacey with a knowing grin. "I admit if you would have told me the two of you were seeing each other that would have given me concern, considering Eli's reputation. But asking you to marry him is serious. Shows you mean a lot to him, and I'm happy for the both of you."

"Thanks," Eli said, smiling. "And I want you to leave Phoenix knowing Stacey is in good hands. I intend to take good care of her and treat her the way she deserves to be treated."

A huge grin appeared on Cohen's face. "That's good to know." Cohen then shook Eli's hand before hugging his sister and congratulating them both.

Galen and Brittany then approached. A genuine smile lit his brother's eyes and Eli couldn't help but nod. He hated to admit it but Galen's prediction had come true. Eli had figured things out before the wedding.

Chapter 18

"I think tonight went well," Eli said as he led Stacey into his home and closed the door behind them.

"Yes, it did."

Since Stacey had been the hostess they had hung back until everyone had left and had helped straighten up. Dee had helped while Eli had gotten a chance to talk to Cohen one-on-one. Eli was confident that he had effectively squashed any concerns or misgivings Cohen might have had regarding his relationship with Stacey, and he felt pretty good about it.

Eli frowned thinking his brothers were another matter. All but Galen were being downright difficult. They saw his defection as a threat to their way of life. First Galen and then him. The possibility that they weren't immune to falling in love like they'd assumed had them literally terrified. He chuckled knowing their time would eventually come. If it could happen to him then it could happen to anyone.

"But I hated lying to everyone. What happens when they find out the truth?" Stacey interrupted his thoughts to ask.

He turned and watched her drop down on his sofa and cross her legs. "And what do you think is the truth that they will find out?" he asked her.

She ran her fingers through the curls on her head and he wasn't surprised that he found such a simple act so sensuous. "That we aren't in love and that our decision to marry was strictly business." She nibbled on her bottom lip thoughtfully and then added, "I wished you hadn't laid things on so thick."

He smiled, knowing just what she was referring to. Once the announcement was made he hadn't wasted any time showing how he felt about her. He knew it had been there in the way he'd looked at her, the way he touched her. He had even kissed her a few times in front of everyone, giving the impression that he adored his fiancée and looked forward to a wedding. He knew Stacey assumed he was playacting. She would be shocked to discover he hadn't been.

He dropped down on the sofa beside her and lifted her legs to place them across his lap. "I couldn't help it. You shouldn't be so tempting," he said, proceeding to remove the sandals from her feet.

"You took advantage of the situation."

He chuckled as he dropped one of her shoes to the floor, which within seconds was followed by the other. "I plead the fifth."

She threw her head back and laughed. "You would."

When her laughter subsided, she smiled and said, "Your mother seemed happy."

He chuckled again. "Trust me, it wasn't an act. Nothing would make her happier than for each of her sons to marry. We made her extremely happy tonight." And he honestly knew they had.

"She invited me to dinner with the family on Thursday," she said softly.

He glanced over at her. "You don't want to go?"

"I'll go but it will only compound the lies. More playacting."

He bit down on his lip, tempted to tell her how he felt but he knew to do so would make her bolt. Cohen had even expressed his surprise that his sister had fallen in love again after vowing she never would. Only Eli knew she hadn't yet fallen in love. But he was determined to do everything in his power to make sure she did. Right now she was sexually attracted to him. Lust, pure and simple. But he was a living witness that with the right person, lust could be transformed into love. It had happened with Galen, it had happened to him and he was determined that it would happen to Stacey.

"Dee didn't seem to mind that you won't be returning to your place tonight," he said.

She smiled. "No, and chances are she won't be returning there either. If she has her way she'll be going home with Cohen tonight. She has loved him forever and has finally gotten the courage to do something about it."

Eli reached up and began running his fingers through her curls, like he'd seen her do earlier. She said nothing, but merely closed her eyes to bask in his ministrations. God, he loved her. How could he have thought that he didn't? However, there was one thing bothering him.

"Your ring."

She opened her eyes and looked over at him. "What about it?"

"Don't you like it?"

Her eyes widened. "Don't I like it? A ring by Zion. Are you kidding?" She held her hand out in front of her and stared at it. "I love it! It's *my* ring. I actually saw it in that jeweler window one day and wished it was mine. To find out it really is sent me in one crazy tail-spin. And because I saw it in that window and it's a ring by Zion, I can imagine how much it cost. The fact that you spent that much on a ring that I'll end up keeping is simply mind-boggling."

He chuckled, glad he'd read her wrong earlier when he thought she hadn't liked it. "I told you I was generous."

She smiled as she slid closer to him. "Yes, you did." She reached up and wrapped her arms around his neck. "And I find your generosity contagious. Let me show you how much."

She then pulled his mouth down to hers.

Stacey slowly opened her eyes as sunlight came in through the window and shifted in bed to discover she was alone. She stretched as memories of the night before came flooding down on her. Pretending or not, she had thoroughly enjoyed the attention Eli had bestowed upon her in front of everyone. He had made her feel significant, special and loved.

Loved.

She shook off the thought and knew love had nothing to do with it. Love was not driving Eli. Love was not why she was wearing one heck of rock on her finger. Love had nothing to do with her being sexually satisfied this morning after a night of making love nonstop.

It was lust and not love.

And it also had to do with all Eli's ambitions in life and taking control and making sure he succeed in everything he wanted. Right now he wanted to be the president of that business council.

His mother was excited they would be having a Christmas wedding and had offered to help her with the guest list like she had Brittany. Similar to Brittany, Stacey was motherless, but Stacey had a feeling Eden Steele would remedy that and become the mother she'd lost. She appreciated the woman's help and attention and felt bad it would only be temporary.

She knew now that breaking up with Eli would be the hardest thing she'd ever have to do, because, regardless of her vow never to believe in fairy tales or forever-after, a part of her was compelled to do so again…because of the ring on her finger. Looking at it, seeing it on her hand, remembering him putting it there was making her accept what she'd been fighting for the past few weeks.

She had fallen in love with Eli.

That had been the last thing she'd wanted but she didn't have to think hard as to how it happened. Each and every time they made love he would take a little piece of her heart although she knew he wasn't sharing any of his. That was fine. Loving him was something she would work hard to get over. She knew the score with him. He'd been up-front from the beginning. It was about sex and nothing more. No emotional entanglements. That thought was uppermost in her mind when she shifted positions and drifted back to sleep.

But emotions she hadn't counted on had sneaked into the picture and the ring on her finger hadn't helped. It might not have any significant meaning for him but it did for her.

Loving him wasn't something she would eventually work out of her system—at least not any time soon. So what was she going to do? How was she going to stay with him knowing how much it would hurt when their marriage ended and he sent her away? The pain would be worse than what she had endured with Wallace. Why had she allowed herself to fall in love with Eli? Why was she setting herself up for more heartbreak?

The answer was simple. She hadn't been able to help herself. She had been warned those "Bad News" Steeles were irresistible; she just hadn't known how irresistible they were.

Eli grabbed his cell phone on the single ring and smiled when he saw the caller ID. "News definitely gets around in this family," he said to his cousin Donovan, who was calling from Charlotte.

Donovan Ridge Steele laughed. "It's good to hear another of Drew's boys has bit the dust. Two down, four to go."

"You better not let Tyson, Jonas, Mercury and Gannon hear you say that."

"Hey, that's what they get for acting like they did when they heard I'd gotten engaged," Donovan said.

Eli remembered that time over two years ago. He had been one of those bachelor Steeles who'd taken Donovan's engagement as a personal affront. Donovan had been their older cousin and their hero since his womanizing ways had been legendary. So much so that a lot of people assumed he had to be one of Drew's boys.

"I understand it will be a Christmas wedding," Donovan said.

"Yes, so pass the word among the family. I want everyone here."

Donovan laughed again. "To see another one of Drew's boys tie the knot, they wouldn't miss it."

A short while later Eli had ended the call with Donovan, which had been followed by calls from his other cousins in Charlotte, all sending congratulations his way. He glanced at the clock on the wall. Stacey was still sleeping and he felt she deserved her rest. He had a couple of cases he could work on so he moved toward his office to do just that.

He grabbed his coffee cup and was about to go into his study when there was a knock at his door. He had a feeling who his early-morning visitors were. He shook his head. They hadn't wasted any time seeking him out.

He opened the door and smiled down their frowns. "Good morning," he said cheerfully. "I hope one of you brought breakfast because I am starving."

Eli stared at his brothers across the table. Jonas had brought breakfast for everyone and they'd all dug in, deciding they would eat first and curse him out later.

Not surprisingly, it was Tyson who spoke up first. "You know what Cohen should have done was kick your you-know-what for messing around with Stacey behind his back in the first place."

"And I should have suspected something was up when I saw the way you were looking at her that day at Ireland when we got together after work to celebrate Cohen's promotion. You were probably involved with her then."

Eli remembered that day. They had kissed earlier at her shop, so, yes, he definitely had been involved with her. "Yes," he said to Jonas, taking a sip of his coffee. "I was involved with her then."

"And you didn't tell anyone?" Mercury accused. "Why did you keep it a secret?"

"I knew how you guys would probably freak out about it. Besides, I didn't want Mom getting her hopes up in case things didn't work out," he said, knowing those reasons sounded plausible.

"Well, we don't like you pulling a Galen on us," Gannon grumbled. "You know what Mom thinks this means."

Eli shrugged. "She will only think that way if you all let her. In fact, all of you should be thanking me. She'll be so busy helping Stacey plan our wedding that she won't have time to harass any of you for a while."

Smiles lit the faces of his brothers as they considered what he'd said. "Umm, you do have a point there," Gannon said. Then his eyes narrowed as he asked, "Why the rush to get married on Christmas Day?"

That answer was easy. "Because I want to start the New Year off right with Stacey as my wife."

They didn't say anything, just stared at him as if they were trying to determine the sincerity of his words. Not wanting them to think too long and hard, he quickly spoke up. "Donovan called. The Charlotte Steeles have heard about it already."

Mercury rolled his eyes. "Mom's doing. I bet she was on the phone before the party ended."

"Probably," they all agreed simultaneously.

Eli glanced at his watch. "I hate to rush you guys off, but I have a house guest that I'd like to spend some time with today."

His announcement that Stacey was somewhere under his roof brought out his brothers' frowns again. "You better do right by her, Eli," Tyson said in a snarl.

Eli waved off his brother's words. "It might take a Steele a long time to find the perfect woman and fall in love, but when we do, we know how to do the right thing and be dedicated for life. We're Drew's boys in more ways than one."

Chapter 19

Stacey took a sip of her wine and smiled up at the older gentleman who Eli had introduced her to moments earlier. She liked Harry Farmer. He was a lovable old man who didn't mind telling that he was still in love with his wife of almost fifty years, was proud of the three children she'd given him and that he simply adored his six grandkids. And he'd even gone on to say that now that Eli had shown he'd matured and settled down he would throw his support Eli's way for the office of president of the business council.

She continued to smile although deep inside, her heart was breaking, something she'd sworn she would never let happen to her again. But she hadn't counted on a man like Eli entering her life and taking over her mind, body, soul, but most important, her heart.

It had been two weeks since the night they'd officially announced their engagement and they'd rarely spent any time apart since. She spent a lot of nights over at his place and they usually made love before sharing a ride to work. Then in the afternoons, they would ride home together. On occasion they'd gone to movies, dinners and concerts in the afternoons. He even had season tickets to football games. She would have to admit that she enjoyed their time together immensely.

At times, Stacey felt she should submit Eli's name to the Academy to be nominated for an Oscar. He was definitely playing the part of a love-smitten fiancé. No matter where they went or who they were with, if you didn't know any better—and most people didn't—you would assume he was a man deeply in love. Sad thing was that she did know better. Eli did not truly love her. He was only acting.

But she was not. Whenever they made love she put her heart, body and soul into it. Even when she was with him meeting his friends and other family members, she was sincere when she expressed her love for him. Only thing, he would never know just how sincere she was.

Even Eden and Brittany had won special places in her heart. Both had welcomed her to the family and offered their services in helping her plan the wedding, which was less than a month away. Tonight they were attending the business council's annual Thanksgiving party. All Eli's brothers, except for Tyson, were entrepreneurs and were in attendance. His parents were attending as well. Although Drew had turned the running of his trucking company over to Gannon, Drew was still somewhat involved.

"You okay?" Eli asked her moments later when

Harry Farmer had moved on and they were standing alone.

She glanced up at him. "Yes, I'm fine."

She was lying. In all truth she wasn't. People would often stop by to comment that they made a beautiful couple and to wish them well on their upcoming marriage. She would smile and thank them while knowing their well wishes were for nothing.

"It seems everyone loves your ring," he whispered close to her ear.

She smiled as she gazed down at her hand. Several women *had* complimented her about her ring. It was definitely an attention getter. "I can see why, Eli, it's beautiful."

"And it was meant just for you. It's a ring that a man would give the woman he loves."

Then why am I wearing it? She was tempted to ask. Instead, she glanced around before looking back at him. "We're alone, Eli. You don't have to say something like that to me now."

"Yes, I do."

She glanced up, giving him a questioning look when a voice behind them cut in. "Well, well, if it isn't Eli, the stud."

Eli glared at the woman standing in front of him at the same time he wrapped his arms around Stacey's waist to bring her closer into his arms. "Liz, what are you doing here?" He of all people knew how vindictive his former lover could be.

"Same thing as you," the woman said haughtily. "I had no idea you would be here tonight."

Eli knew she was lying through her teeth. "Fine. Now you know. Please make it your business to keep your distance." The last time he'd seen her he had threatened her with a restraining order if she didn't curtail her stalking tendencies.

"Touchy, aren't you?" She then glanced over at Stacey and sneered. "You don't know me, however, I can't help but notice your ring. If it's what I think it is, then my advice is for you to think twice about it. Eli Steele is not the marrying kind so if I were you, I'd wonder what's in it for him."

To Eli's surprise, Stacey chuckled. He glanced down at her and saw the way she lifted her chin and stiffened her spine. "Oh, I can tell you what's in it for him. I'm in it for him. He'll be getting *me*. Do yourself a favor and don't run behind a man who evidently doesn't want you. Now if you'll excuse us."

Taking his hand, they walked off leaving Liz standing there, speechless.

Eli opened the door to his home trying hard to decipher Stacey's mood. She hadn't said much on the ride home and had been awfully quiet. Although she had put Liz in her place tonight, he had a feeling she wasn't happy about it. And he had an even stronger feeling that she was upset. Mainly with him.

He closed the door behind them and when she headed off toward the bedroom he reached out and snagged her hand. "I think we need to talk."

"What about?"

"What happened tonight at the party with Liz."

She waved off his suggestion with her other hand.

"No need. I think my performance took care of it. Your bid for the presidency is still safe, Eli."

He released her hand and slid his into his pocket as irritation rushed through him. "Do you think that's all I care about? Becoming president of the business council?"

She appeared confused by his question. "Yes, of course. What else do you care about?"

He knew she wasn't intentionally trying to come off as a smart aleck. She actually believed what she was saying, and he couldn't very much blame her for thinking that way since he'd given her no reason to think otherwise. "Plenty, and I think we need to talk about just what those things are," he said, leaning against the door.

She sighed deeply, wearily. "There's nothing to talk about, Eli. If you're worried what that woman said has upset me, then don't be. I've known that you are a man who is truly not the marrying kind. That isn't a secret. I also know what I agreed to do and that what we have is a business arrangement and nothing more."

She paused a moment and then added softly, "What she said is true. There is something in it for you and I'm okay with it. Because in the end I'll take the same advice I gave her. I don't intend to run behind a man who doesn't want me."

Her words gave him pause. Was that a hint that perhaps she had feelings for him but assumed he didn't have any for her? He moved away from the door to come stand in front of her and placed his hands at her waist. "And what if I said that I wanted you?"

She rolled her eyes. "You always want me. It's been that way between us from the start."

That was true. "Then what if I said I want the one thing that you don't want?" he asked.

"Which is?"

"An emotional entanglement."

She didn't say anything for a moment as her brow furrowed. And then she asked, "And what's your definition of an emotional entanglement?"

"It involves a relationship that goes beyond the bedroom."

She stared at him a moment and then she shook her head like she didn't believe him. "Why? Why would you want something like that?"

He had no trouble telling her the reason and hoped to God that she believed him. "Because I've fallen in love with you, Stacey. And since we seem to communicate on more of a physical level than an emotional one, I'm going to show you just what I mean."

Stacey was silent, basically in a daze as she watched Eli begin removing his clothes. First he eased his jacket off his massive shoulders and tossed it aside at the same time he kicked off his shoes. He then began unbuttoning his shirt.

She was stunned by his actions as well as by the words he'd just spoken. Had he just said he had fallen in love with her? She shook her head as if to clear it, while thinking she was definitely hearing things. There was no way he loved her. She tried to focus on what he was doing, watching as he jerked the tail of his shirt from his slacks.

"You heard me right," he said, as if reading her thoughts. By now his hand was tugging his pants down a pair of powerful-looking thighs, thighs that had ridden her numerous times to more orgasms than she could count. Shivers rushed through her at the memories.

"That night I asked you again to marry me out on Tyson's patio, I had a reason for doing so. The first time I asked you to marry me was for all the wrong reasons. That night I asked you for the right one. And if you recall, I told you I loved you that night was well. I meant it then and I mean it now. I realized it the moment I walked into Cohen's party and saw you. It hit me like a ton of bricks but it hit me nonetheless. My head couldn't deny what my heart was saying."

When he was completely naked he reached out and pulled her into his arms and captured her mouth. He silenced the *Oh* off her lips in a hot, open-mouth kiss that she felt in every part of her body, especially in the area at the juncture of her thighs.

She recalled very little after that, especially when he removed the clothes off her body as quickly and efficiently as only he knew how to do. And when he had stripped her of every single piece, he swept her off her feet into his arms and headed for the bedroom.

The moment their bodies connected on the bed, they made love uncontrollably. Whatever snapped inside of Eli snapped inside of Stacey as well. Desire stroked all over her skin and his tongue followed, licking her, tasting her, driving her over the edge and then snatching her back right before she could tumble.

The nipples of her breasts stiffened even more under

the assault of his practiced tongue and the area between her legs was wet from the attention of his fingers. Moments later his mouth replaced his fingers and she screamed out his name.

"Eli!"

"I'm here, baby, and I don't intend on leaving you or letting you leave me," he whispered huskily.

And then he was pulling her up on all fours and her pulse quickened, her heart pounded in her chest and heat rushed through her bloodstream when he hovered behind her, grinding his hips against her rounded backside. She felt all of him, as he rubbed his shaft over her hips, seeking the entry to her womanhood from behind.

He found it and she felt the heat of his chest on her back when he mounted her that way, his strong legs and thick thighs locking her body to his. "I love making love to you, Stacey," he whispered in a heated breath close to her ear. "But even more important is that I love you in every way a man can possibly love a woman, even this way. Feel the love. Feel the emotional entanglement."

And then he thrust inside of her wrapping his arms around her in such a way that her hips were rendered immobile. He began pounding into her hard. Fast. Deep.

Eli gritted his teeth as he continued to make love to Stacey, frantically, desperately and wildly. Nothing could have prepared him for the intensity of this lovemaking and he knew as feverish as what they were doing was, they were not having sex. They were making love. They would always make love when they came together this way.

And then an explosion hit her body. The satiny cheeks of her backside began to tremble in a force that nearly bucked him off her. But he held on, continued to thrust inside of her. And when she screamed his name, his body reacted and he erupted and kept on coming inside the woman he loved. The only woman he could ever love.

When she screamed his name again, he knew there was no way she could assume there was no emotional entanglement between them again.

Stacey couldn't move. Even when Eli lowered her body down on the bed then joined her to wrap her into his arms, she was too exhausted to do anything but breathe and that was barely. OMG. That had to be love-making at its most intense. Now her body felt limp, drained but totally satisfied.

"Did I make my point?"

She heard Eli's question but was too weak to lift her head to gaze at him. Yes, he had made his point, although it was still hard for her to believe. "You love me," she said in a voice that still sounded stunned.

"Yes, I love you and one day I will hear you tell me that you love me back."

Stacey fought back the tears as she garnered the strength to lift her head to stare into the beauty of his green eyes. "I love you, Eli. I love you so much and not in a million years did I think you could love me back. I had accepted the kind of marriage we would have and knew after that year I would walk away. I wouldn't be like Liz and run behind a man who didn't want me."

He reached out and caressed the side of her face with

his fingers. "Now you know how much I want you and just how much I love you. To me, one is just as strong as the other. You are my life and on Christmas Day I intend to make you my forever wife."

"So I'll get a Steele for Christmas," she said as her lips curled into a happy smile.

"Baby, you'll have a Steele for the rest of your life. That, I promise you." And then he lowered his head and captured her lips, sealing the vow he'd just made.

Epilogue

Christmas Day

Eli glanced around the room where his wedding reception was being held. The Steeles liked getting together and when the reason was a wedding, that made things even better. The small wedding he and Stacey planned had gotten kicked by the wayside when a number of people wanted to witness for themselves another one of Drew's boys being taken off the bachelor list.

He looked over at his four remaining single brothers who were standing across the room with their cousin Vanessa, her husband, Cameron, and their eight-month-old son, Steele Cameron Cody. They had gotten over their irritation with him since they all liked Stacey. Besides, since all four were convinced what happened to him and Galen was a fluke and in no way would happen to them, they felt safe and secure in their bachelor status.

At the rehearsal dinner last night, his cousin Taylor had announced that she and her husband Dominic were expecting another child in the summertime, and everyone had celebrated that good news. And it was good to hear that Marcus, their cousin Chance's oldest son was doing well at the university and had decided to go to law school. Eli was pleased to hear that.

Eli's gaze shifted to his parents, namely his mother. She was happy. She'd been able to bag two daughters-in-law within a year's time. That wasn't bad. His marriage to Stacey had given his single brothers a slight reprieve, but he'd warned them not to get too comfortable. Their mother wouldn't be satisfied until they were all happily married.

He shifted his gaze yet again to come to rest on Cohen, who was talking to Dee. He remembered what Stacey had told him about the couple, but for some reason, they didn't seem too happy with each other now. He wondered what was going on with that.

He glanced down at his watch. Stacey had gone upstairs to change. They would be leaving for Paris in a few hours. Every time he thought about the fact that she was legally his wife, he felt a rush of heat consume him. She was everything he could possibly want in a woman.

A few days ago, he had presented her with a huge treasure chest and when she'd opened it she looked at him confused. Until he had explained that all the items inside the chest had been things he'd purchased from her shop for no apparent reason, other than to pretend he wanted to buy something just to see her. There were magazines he hadn't read, candy bars he'd never eaten and a lot of other miscellaneous items that had probably totaled up to a lot of money that he didn't consider as wasted. Seeing all the items collected made him realize that he had loved her even then.

And then he couldn't help but chuckle at the time a couple of weeks ago when he and Stacey had traveled to Memphis to attend Dee's parents' anniversary party. He had made sure everyone, especially Wallace and Gail, had known just how much he loved and adored Stacey. He was certain he hadn't left any doubt in anyone's mind that not marrying Wallace Flowers was the best thing she could have done and the man really had done her a favor.

"Looking for me?"

He turned and smiled. His wife had surprised him and come from behind. He raked his gaze up and down her outfit. She was wearing a cute short red dress and a pair of black leather boots. Since he'd told her how much he enjoyed seeing her legs, she made it a point to show them to him every chance she got.

"Yes, I was looking for you," he said, pulling her into his arms. "Are you ready to start our honeymoon, sweetheart?"

She wrapped her arms around his neck. "Yes, I'm more than ready."

He lowered his head and kissed her and knew it was just one of many they would share during their lifetime together.

* * * * *

Every woman
wants him.
But he wants
only her…
New York Times
and USA TODAY
bestselling author
BRENDA
JACKSON
KIMANI ROMANCE
NEW YORK TIMES AND USA TODAY BESTSELLING AUTHOR
BRENDA
JACKSON
BACHELOR
UNDONE
BACHELORS
IN DEMAND

KIMANI
ROMANCE
TM